Diverse Voices
Reunited

Bulkington Writers

Edited by
Hazel McLoughlin

Produced by
Tony Rattigan

INTRODUCTION

Despite the "unprecedented times" imposed by the lockdown restrictions of the covid pandemic and the sad announcement from Diane Lindsay that she would not be returning to teach her longstanding Creative Writing Class, Bulkington Writers have felt inspired to re-emerge, reconvene and reunite.

We are now a Writing Group who meet weekly to read our own work and offer supportive criticism to others.

We are a disparate group - diverse writers - with a broad variety of style and voice but united in our motivation to write and our need for an audience.

We hope you will enjoy what we offer in this anthology.

CONTENTS

THE GHOST WALK 1

AUTUMN 7

A PATH THROUGH THE WOOD 9

ON DEMENTIA 17

THE FAMILY HOUSE 18

MUCH ADO ABOUT NOTHING 25

REST HOME RHYTHM AND BLUES 33

TRANSGRESSION 35

NO, THAT'S SPELT G-U-I-D-O 38

THE COMMUTE 42

A TRANQUIL SEA 49

PIE DANCE 57

ORPHEUS IN THE UNDERGROUND 59

BARNEY THE BASSETT HOUND 62

BOOKWORM 65

A PTOLEMAIC TALE 69

LOVERS REUNITED 81

ROGUE ELEMENT 83

SPACE 88

IN A WIDE OPEN SPACE 89

THE GRAND NATIONAL 94

THE HOUSE 115

McGONAGALL'S GHOST 117

FRANCOPHONE 134

ONE NIGHT IN BANGOR 138

COLD WHITE HORSE 145

ENCOUNTERS 146

THE THEATRE VISIT 155

THE RAIN 157

ETERNAL NIGHT 159

RISING DAWN 162

LAST REQUEST 167

THE GHOST WALK

Sue Tompkinson

It seems as if Charlie has been telling the same tales and following the same paths around Pebblesey Cove forever. In fact, it's been only six years but repetition has a habit of magnifying the perception of time. With long thick overcoat and felt fedora, he cuts a somewhat dashing figure of theatrical elegance. His rich sonorous voice can, in one breath, project from one end of town to the other and then, without warning, fall to the merest whisper. Not only does he sound the part but at six feet four inches tall, he defies anyone to question any word he utters.

He looks around at the growing crowd huddled together for warmth, this being the start of dank autumn days before the chill of winter takes hold. It's the season when coach-loads of retired trippers have time on their hands to avoid the clash of boisterous kids during school holidays. The day hasn't quite dissolved into dusk at this vantage point on High Cliff and Charlie waits just long enough to let the tension mount before addressing the assembled crowd eager, as always, to be scared witless, poked fun at and generally entertained.

'Good afternoon everyone, or should I say good evening? I believe at this hour we fall betwixt those two moments in time.'

Charlie sweeps the horizon with outstretched hand, 'Welcome, one and all, to the beautiful harbour town of Pebblesey Cove, a town that is full of glorious scenery, fascinating history, and a plethora of weird and wonderful characters - both past and present!' Everyone laughs as pointedly he looks around, insinuating that present company is definitely included.

And so, he starts telling the first of his many tales to the silent, awestruck holidaymakers, brave enough to endure the falling temperature. As he does so, his concentration is broken by some shuffling at the back of the crowd. An elderly woman and her young male companion, arms linked, separate at once. The young man goes to grab her arm, not in a friendly way but almost desperate in manner. Charlie assumes he must be her son, or perhaps grandson, maybe suffering a complaint that makes him rely heavily on her care. But then, to Charlie's complete surprise, she places her hand over the young man's face and pushes him away. Unbelievable, he thinks, and immediately interrupts his story to ask if everything is alright.

The woman smiles and says, 'Fine thank you, just feeling a bit cold.' Then a change in tone as she stamps her feet.

'I'll be better when we start moving.'

As everyone's looking in Charlie's direction, they haven't noticed anything amiss. All seems calm once more, so Charlie shrugs his shoulders and swings the interruption to his advantage, drawing in the crowd again with practised ease. As they walk along, Charlie loses sight of the young man and elderly woman, but he has been lucky enough to encourage a large crowd today so it's not unusual to lose sight of whole swathes of followers however many times he tells them to "keep together now". So far, he hasn't lost anyone permanently.

The tour takes them full-circle returning, for the final chilling farewell, to High Cliff, overlooking the now glittering lights below. It is at this stage in the proceedings that Charlie hands out flyers for his itinerary of tours and presentations throughout the coming days and weeks. Just as the crowd starts to break away, he remembers the disquiet he felt earlier and seeks out the elderly lady and her young companion to satisfy himself that all is well. As she appears to be on her own now, he tries, as diplomatically as he can, to ask about the young man.

'Your son decided not to join us then? Must admit, I can be a bit scary sometimes,' Charlie laughs nervously.

She gives him a puzzled look and quite smartly suggests that he's obviously been telling ghost stories for far too long and is perhaps in need of a holiday himself.

'I don't have a son - or a daughter for that matter,' she tells him.

'Oh, I just assumed - I meant the young man you were with....?'

'What young man? I don't know what you're talking about. I travel alone - there *is* no young man. And I don't need any more bits of paper, thank you very much.'

'Of course. I'm so sorry. I must be confused.' Charlie is confused.

'Didn't mean to upset you Madam. I do hope you enjoyed the tour.' And as he effects a mock bow, she drifts away to join the rest of the coach party heading back to the hotel, more than ready for their evening meal.

***

Charlie ponders the mystery and starts to doubt himself as he sits in the near empty bar, soothing his well-used vocal chords with a second pint. As he returns to his table, a man he recognises from the tour comes up to him.

'Mind if I join you, or have you had enough of us lot for one day?' The man introduces himself as Bill.

'No. Please,' says Charlie, motioning towards the table where he had left his coat and hat.

'I'd be happy for the company. Enjoy the tour, did you, or were you just along for the ride - keeping the missus happy?'

'Nay, lad. You did a good job there. Very entertaining you were - and funny with it. I'd ask if all the tales were true, but best not, eh?' Bill says with a wink.

Charlie smiles. 'I take it you're with the Yorkshire coach tour then?'

'That's right. Always put on a good trip, d'they. Good hotel, plenty of days out. No, can't complain 'bout them, that's for sure.'

'Tell me,' says Charlie, 'the elderly lady in the green coat and brown hat, is she with your party - glasses and large scarf?'

Bill thinks for a minute and then realises who Charlie means.

'That'll be Doreen. Aye, Doreen. She's alright, I suppose - a bit of a sharp tongue at times though.'

'Know her well, do you Bill?'

'No, not really. Why do you ask?'

'Hope I'm not speaking out of turn,' says Charlie, 'but I just wondered if she gets a bit confused sometimes. Thought she was with a young companion, but could be wrong.'

'No odds t' me lad, no relation of mine. Can't say I've noticed anyone with her though, but I'll tell you something - she's as sharp as a tack and that's a fact. Yon lass on Reception got a right flea in her ear when she charged her for a paper she hadn't ordered. Careful with her pennies, I reckon, is our Doreen. Had a sad old life though, by all accounts.'

'Oh yes, why's that then?' Charlie, more interested than he cares to let on.

'Well, she were telling a group of us t'other evening - when the subject of husbands came up - that her first husband died just a few days after the marriage ceremony. On honeymoon, would you believe? Tragic it were, just tragic. Mind you, I did have some knowledge of mishap, though I didn't let on. Thought I'd let her take stage, so to speak.'

'So what happened?' asks Charlie.

'Well, apparently he - her husband, that is - liked to do a bit of fishing. They'd gone to Lake District after nuptials for that very purpose. They'd taken out a small boat on one o' the Lakes - can't remember which one she said just now. Anyways, she settled to read her book while he cast his line. Then, as he reached up in excitement of a possible catch, he took a fainting fit. Did no more than fall int' water in process. She grabbed his arm, like, but weren't strong enough to haul him back into the boat, and no one in sight, she says. Of course, yon mobiles were still a thing of the future, weren't they. Over an hour she held onto him until both were so exhausted that he just slipped away into water. Like I say, tragic. By time someone spotted her distress, it were all too late.'

'Poor woman,' says Charlie, shaking his head, 'I'm surprised she can bear to talk about it.'

'Oh I don't think that bothers her. Quite graphic it were really.' Bill leans forward and touches the side of his nose.

'I think she enjoys the attention, m'self, not to mention shocking t'other ladies. One thing though, reckon he left her well provided for, not that she lets on, of course, but wife's cousin knew him, see. Well, he'd heard of him, let's say. Bit of a name in local business, so it goes, even though he were no age. Inherited a couple of factories apparently, finger in plenty of pies if you get my drift. So at least she wasn't left a pauper. Beats me why she comes on these cheap coach trips. Could all be a front, of course.

She might just like clinging onto her brass and playing the poor widow. Who knows?'

'A front? Yes indeed,' murmurs Charlie.

'You may've hit the nail on the head there, Bill.'

A cold shudder runs down Charlie's spine as the scene he'd witnessed earlier plays back to him. The distraught look of the young man as he tried to grab her arm ... her hand clasped over his face as she pushed him away ... It suddenly becomes quite vivid again.

Bill interrupts his thoughts.

'In fact, she did go on t'say that she'd had two more husbands - after first poor beggar, like - *and* she'd managed to outlive the both of 'em! They do say women generally live longer than men, don't they?'

'They do, Bill, that they do. Fancy joining this confirmed bachelor in a whisky? I'm feeling the cold all of a sudden.'

AUTUMN

Jean Busby

When I hear Nigel Kennedy's CD as he plays, 'Autumn,' from the 'Four Seasons,' there is a certain magic about it. One of my favourite seasons is autumn. When walking through a wood it always fascinates me how the leaves on the trees change from green to gold, yellow and red colours. They seem to stand out like a bright sunbeam. Although the leaves eventually fall to the ground leaving the branches bare there is a certain beauty to behold.

In the 1980's my family were very fortunate to live in Connecticut, USA. During the autumn season we used to drive as far as Stowe to follow the famous fall trail experiencing the beautiful colours throughout the states.

The Highlands of Scotland is a lovely place to visit showing an array of colours, as is The National Arboretum Forest in Gloucestershire. Most National Trust grounds show these wonderful colours of the trees and shrubs.

Of course, autumn is also the harvest season whereby our farmers begin to gather corn crops and vegetables to prepare for the winter months. Apples and other fruits are harvested in the orchards. Grapes are picked from the vines to be made into wine.

People who belong to Sunday school and Church prepare baskets laden with fruit and vegetables. Home-made bread shaped like a sheaf of corn is placed in the centre of the aisle, the baskets are placed each side of this. After a blessing most of these items are auctioned off to raise money for charity. The Village Institutes hold fruit and vegetable competitions to celebrate harvest.

As the weather becomes cooler there is less dust in the air and everywhere seems fresher. The days seem to become shorter and as the nights draw in people think that Christmas is not very far away. Autumn and winter clothes are changed from our summer clothes.

Some children beginning the autumn term at a new school are excited, others anxious not knowing what to expect.

Swallows and starlings fly away to warmer countries and then return in our warmer season. Sadly whilst our garden plants of summer are losing their bloom and dying off, our shrubs are still quite colourful. But the blackbirds and robins never fly away and we can still hear them chirping merrily away throughout autumn and winter.

A PATH THROUGH THE WOOD

June Bradley

It had always been his favourite season. As a child he waited patiently each year for autumn and its harvest of fruit, deposited generously from the horse chestnut tree in the field behind the house. Every morning before school he would search the carpet of leaves at the end of the garden for conkers. He was seventeen and about to leave home for university before he managed to beat his father at the game. Happy times. Sweet memories.

The sun was still low and the air untainted by the day when Leo pulled away from the house having deposited both his suitcase and the dog in the back of his old jeep and his rucksack on the passenger seat. He glanced in the rear view mirror at Sadie's new 'Cardinal Red, showroom fresh Mercedes Sports Coupe' now resplendent in sole occupancy of the drive. He smiled to himself as he turned out of the road and it disappeared from view. It felt good that there would be no return journey. As he headed for the bypass out of the city he took a deep breath and relaxed his shoulders.

He knew it was as much his fault as Sadie's to begin with. She was twelve years his junior when they first met, vibrant, feisty and driven with a passionate nature he was too weak to deny. She had a look of the exotic and once told him her grandmother had been Brazilian but it was just one of the many claims he had never been able to confirm. Up there with the fervent denials of infidelity in their relationship and unrecorded transactions in the business they ran together. Up there with the claim that she had miscarried the baby who had prompted their marriage. Up there with the tearful admission that the doctor had told her she would never be able to conceive again, without her knowing Leo had found an empty pack of contraceptive pills several years later, labelled with her name and address, on the ground after the bin collection one morning. He had once thought her beautiful and to the untrained eye she still was, but now there was almost a brittleness about it. What used to be a seductive pout had developed into an unattractive sneer, an upward tilt of her chin was no longer accompanied by a teasing smile, it had developed into a signal of dismissal or a sign of contempt.

Many things were breakable - fine porcelain, crystal glass, contracts and oh yes, trust. Leo often wondered if a heart could be truly broken, after all Sadie had put his to the test so many times throughout their years together. Like a cobra she could strike with deadly accuracy and speed the venom of her words paralysing the ability to reply. He had ignored the imperceptible creaks and hairline cracks caused by a spiteful remark or thoughtless action from her until one day his heart's warm gentle centre cracked under the weight of her disregard for him. His heart attack, the doctor assured him, was a warning and most likely caused by stress and anxiety. He would not be so lucky next time. A lifestyle change was imperative; he would live his life in his own way and stop this merry-go-round of destructiveness.

He took 'gardening leave' from the business which Sadie surprisingly agreed would be the sensible thing to do. He wasn't into Lycra or gyms and knew he would feel uncomfortable amongst a bunch of muscle bound, competitive narcissists. But he did think some company would help him get to grips with his situation. When he took the puppy home wrapped in its blanket with a few toys and a new blue collar and lead it was the happiest Leo had felt for a long time. Sadie however was none too impressed. As she entered the kitchen she stopped in her tracks.

"Good God, where did you find that?"

Leo bristled but kept his voice steady.

"I got him from the local animal shelter. The doctor told me walking was the best exercise to start with and I thought this little fellow would be good company. He'll make sure I keep myself fit and healthy."

"Most people would have bought a bicycle or joined a gym, but then you're not in that category are you? You could have at least found a more attractive beast. It's as plain as a home-made biscuit."

He scratched the back of the puppy's ear then lifted him out of the blanket on to the floor.

"Looks aren't everything, Sadie."

The puppy yawned, stretched and squatted. Leo smiled as a puddle formed and spread across the gleaming tiles. Her look said everything without a breath being taken. She glared at Leo.

"Keep it out of my way and make sure the place doesn't start smelling like a zoo," she snapped.

As the door slammed and her stilettos echoed down the hall, Leo chuckled. He picked up his new friend and ripped off a length of kitchen roll.

"Nice one son," he whispered into its ear, "Take no notice, it's what I'm learning to do. Besides, I like home-made biscuits."

Small victories.

As Ginger, the bringer of companionship grew, Leo began to realise just how lonely and joyless his life had become and what an important part the dog had played in his recovery. Sadie however had never thawed and Ginger treated her with complete indifference, mainly choosing to ignore her. Such were the small joys in Leo's life, until he joined the Woodland Trust volunteers.

***

Leo indicated onto the slip road and exited the bypass. He heard Ginger yawn and glanced in the rear view mirror as the dog stood up and stretched. He had become as familiar with the journey as his master.

"Almost there boy, not far now," he told him.

Ginger pressed his nose against the window wagging his tail in anticipation. Leo turned into the lane acknowledging the 'Woodland Trust' sign and after five hundred yards parked in a roughly cleared square designated for 'Volunteer Parking'. He switched off the engine and leaned back in his seat. He felt cleansed; he always did in this place. The morning sun filtered through the trees, it warmed his face through the windscreen and he sat bathed in its glow for a few minutes until Ginger, bored with the delay began fidgeting and whining. Leo turned in his seat.

"Ok, are you ready?" The dog barked and wagged his tail, "It's time, let's do this my friend."

He got out of the Jeep and opened the tailgate then pulled out the rolled up waterproof mat and tucked it under one arm. As he slung his old rucksack onto the other shoulder Ginger jumped out. Leo let the door close and locked the car. In spite of the sun it was too cool to abandon his jacket. He zipped it up and watched the leaves dancing in the breeze. They shimmered and sparkled copper, gold, flame and bronze. It took him back to his childhood and the memory made him smile. He breathed in deeply savouring the scents of the wood and laughed out loud as the dog bounded up to him, muzzle smeared with soil and autumns detritus, barking playfully. He patted Gingers flank and ruffled his ears. "Come on boy, today is going to be a good day!"

***

They set off at a brisk pace along the path, his leather walking boots scuffing and churning the covering of summers passing as Ginger foraged for canine treasures. After a while he turned off the path into a clearing dominated by a veteran oak tree affectionately known as 'Old George'. He unrolled the mat and spread it over the deep mattress of leaf mould and its autumnal counterpane that had gathered around the base of the tree, then sat down. Leo with the other members had helped to clear and pollard this section of woodland. It had been a long time since he had felt so useful and so at peace with himself. They were a good bunch, volunteers from all walks of life, friendly and cheerful, humorous and serious when the need arose but all of them happy to give their time to something worthwhile. It was here, on this spot under the oak tree where he got to know his kindred spirit and soul mate, Fran, the repairer of hearts. Not conventionally beautiful with her auburn hair and freckled complexion or her generous mouth that twitched to the left just before she smiled. Her beauty came from within, something he had not experienced for many years.

They met at the animal shelter where she worked three days a week. She listened without interruption while he explained his reasons for wanting to adopt a dog, suggesting a puppy as the bond between them would be built from its earliest memories. It was Fran who chose Ginger from the litter of puppies in the shelter's care at the time. She told him about her voluntary work with the Trust and how it could be good for him and the puppy when he was old enough to mix. After he joined they met again and worked together in the same team most of the time. They became friends, close and confident enough to reveal their life situations both good and bad. He found her the most genuine, thoughtful person he had ever known. She had been widowed ten years before, the result of a car accident caused by her husband's inability to control his alcohol consumption, something she was unable to forgive. They started to meet to walk their dogs when they weren't volunteering, Ginger adored Fran and her elderly dog Henry who seemed to have become a role model for him. And as Fran and Leo's relationship blossomed from friendship to lovers it became clear to him how the past years had been wasted.

He was a kind man, always had been, but Sadie had taken this as a sign of weakness. Weak he may have been, but a fool? Never! Sadie's passion for him had always been conditional, her needs sporadic, a bargaining chip to keep in reserve according to her requirements at the time. Fran's love and affection were given freely, unconditionally without compromise. Her passion for him was a gift, a gift that he accepted and readily returned for as long as she would have him.

Ginger, who had given up foraging, had fallen asleep next to Leo. He lifted his head and sat up wagging his tail. Leo watched her striding across the clearing, old jeans and flowery Wellington boots, her old Barbour unbuttoned over a cream cowl neck sweater.

"Come on Henry!" she called to the plodding Spaniel a few steps behind now being ambushed by Ginger running circles around him with the enthusiasm of youth. She laughed at them and waved to Leo. "What a beautiful day?" she beamed, sitting down beside him. Her kiss was long and leisurely. "I've missed you," she whispered.

Leo returned her kiss then took a Thermos flask from the rucksack and poured coffee for them both. She drank some then bit into a ginger biscuit.

"How was it, did everything go Ok?"

"I think so, I'm sure I'll know for certain by tonight." He replied. "The papers will arrive today, this morning hopefully."

Leo had spent a busy week away from Fran. It was something he had to do, should have done a long time ago but without knowing it, she had given him the strength to move forward and told him she would support him whatever decision he chose to make. Leo had filed for divorce and would hand the business over to Sadie. As much as he had lost any feelings he ever had for her and for many years the only other thing they shared was an address, he knew she would keep the business going. It had become her life and she was covetous of its success. His solicitor strongly advised him to keep his shares and would ensure that Sadie sign an affidavit stating that once the business was transferred to her and the house sold on a seventy thirty split in her favour there would be no further concessions or contact with Leo. It would be a full and final settlement.

"Wow," Fran whispered, "She has no grounds for complaint."

"Well the solicitor has known us both for many years and knows how she ticks, he's confident about everything. If she chooses to fight she is likely to lose more than she gains." He kissed Fran again. "We," he whispered, "will be absolutely fine."

"She's a fool Leo, she doesn't realise what she's thrown away. Her cruelty and lack of respect has fuelled our future happiness and for that she has my eternal gratitude."

They held each other tightly until she released him dabbing at her eyes with a tissue.

"Come on, shall we get moving? Everything's ready at

home, dinner's in the slow cooker so there's plenty of time to get unpacked and settled." She gave him a slow smile.

He helped her up. They re-packed the rucksack and rolled up the mat. It would be a big step for them both but they would tread the path together. The journey would begin today.

ON DEMENTIA

Sue Tompkinson

Catch before it falls
the sun upon the land.

Catch before it falls
a snowflake in the hand.

Catch before it falls
pure birdsong on the air.

Catch before it falls
the lovers' languid stare.

Catch before it falls
a nature sweet and kind.

Catch before it falls
the finest, sharpest mind.

Yet my fingers slipped.
I tried to stay your fall.

Too lost now to catch
my raw and anguished call.

THE FAMILY HOUSE

Sue Tompkinson

I love this house, always have, always will, a happy home for the most part. Of course, that's not t' say every memory's a good one. Sure that wouldn't be natural. Haven't we all got something to grieve over? Poor baby Roisin, the tiniest wee coffin I ever did see. Such sorrow leaves a mark that never will rub out.

Along with the tears though, our home witnessed plenty of laughter, and I still feel the warm hug of a welcome when I walk in. Here's the hallway, once cluttered with shoes and boots determined t' trip you up, the cosy front room which Mammy liked to call "the good room", and then the living kitchen that used to be split in two. How she managed in that tiny scullery I'll never know. Upstairs, the two bedrooms have now progressed to one and a half so they can enjoy the company of a small bathroom. It was time to bring that in from the cold, right enough. It may be quieter now after the years of noisy chaos, but every inch of the place bears witness, so it does. And here's me, still in residence, and ever will be if I have anything to do with it.

I suppose it's not the fashion these days t' live your whole life in one place. Don't get me wrong, I have nothin' against an abundance of "get-up-and-go" but I'm happy enough t' leave the upheaval to others. There's a certain comfort in the familiar, so there is. Of course, the young ones are always on at me.

'Why don't ya go travellin' Aunty Carmel? Take in some different air for a change. Sure there's nothin' here

to hold ya back and it'll do ya good, it will.'

I adopt my beatific face and give my usual answer.

'Perhaps one day I might,' which is as bare-faced a lie as you can get. Still, it keeps them quiet, for a while at least.

Will I let you into a secret? But don't be tellin' anyone now! Ya see, I had my future all planned out right here. Well, near here, for the farm's no more than a mile or so as the crow flies. It was my plan to become a farmer's wife. Ah yes, up with the lark feedin' the chicks, then a hot and hearty meal ready each day t' welcome home the love of my life. In the fullness of time, some children perhaps…. Just perfect, me and Padraig, the farmer's son - my future, my destiny. Of course, he made his choice many moons ago and spectacularly burst that bubble, right enough. Whatever he saw in her I'll never know, for plain as a plank she was - compared t' me, that is. I know I shouldn't say this myself, but I was regarded as a good lookin' woman, a real stunner some said. But sure, that was all so long ago and I'm well over him now. At my age? Of course I am. It's just…when I'm not lookin'… the memories sneak up on me and slap me right in the face. I can't understand how such feelings rage on when the rest of me is crumbling away. Doesn't make any sense at all, and I bet if I saw him again after all these years, I'd wonder whatever fired me up in the first place. As it turned out he had no intention of running the farm anyway, and didn't she drag him halfway across the globe soon as the ring was on her finger? Ah, for all I know he could've passed on by now. I don't feel that though, somehow.

Despite the disappointment, I decided to stay put. You see the truth is, I like it here. My childhood was good, certainly it was. Sure, how could I fail t' love the warm cocoon I was brought up in? A big madness of a family, and stunning countryside wrapping itself around me whatever the seasons might bring, be it sunshine, snow or the lovely soft rain. I admit I'm not so fond of the heavy downpours but a good auld storm now, I enjoy the drama in that.

And what a great bunch of pals I had to run around with, even Siobhan and her annoying ways. Always had to be in charge, didn't she, giving out the orders like she knew better. Easier to let her get on with it, that's what we all thought, me and the gang, Marie, Kathleen, Dermot, Vincent. Played out till all hours we did, running and shouting, screeching our heads off. Must have drove folks wild with the noise of us. We turned out okay though. Marie and Dermot teaching, Kathleen a doctor would you believe - she who couldn't stand the sight of blood! Vincent away off lecturing and myself running the local post office. Of course, the one that never grew up, God bless her, was Siobhan herself. Struck down with the cancer she was, before she even reached her teens. She couldn't boss her way out of that one, the poor thing. I often weep at the thought of it, even now. Maybe she's busy sorting them out, up there in heaven. Sure, they wouldn't know what's hit them.

If I'm honest, I did miss my pals when they went off t' study but then, being a part of a big family, I never felt lonely. Besides, I've always managed my own company well enough. There was one occasion, though, when I did pray for help. On this particular day I was on my own in the post office, Sandra having taken herself off to the warehouse, when in burst the Irish version of *"Bonnie and Clyde"*. Okay, so they had sticks instead of guns, and he looked nothing like the actor in the film, but you get the picture. I was well scared so I was, until I realised that behind the piece of rag tied across his face was young Jimmy McCready, spots 'n' all. His young moll was only

Betty Malone, the brazen wee minx. Hadn't I been to her sister's weddin' just the year before? When I addressed the pair of them with their given names, they turned so fast to run away, they nearly knocked each other out. Up they got off the floor and slammed through my shop door like rats through a drainpipe, straight into the loving arms of Garda James McCready, uncle to the would-be gangster himself. I couldn't have written it better if I was making a film.

It's hard t' think I'm the sole occupant now of the family home. Ten of us were squeezed in here at one time - Mammy and Daddy sleeping downstairs and the rest of us upstairs, boys in one room and girls in the other, always arguing over space, as you might imagine. I well remember strutting off t' sleep on the auld blanket chest at the top of the stairs, dragging the counterpane with me for warmth. I chose to ignore the cries from our Lizzy whose bed was now bereft of its cover. You might know, I didn't get a wink of sleep tryin' t' balance myself on the hard auld surface, and I was awarded a parental clip around the ear for my selfish ways.

Talking of our Lizzy, she made a name for herself, didn't she just, doing a disappearing act when she was, what, about twenty-eight I think - old enough to know better anyways. God knows t' this day where she went, and why, but return she did after a couple of weeks gone. We call it her *"Agatha Christie"* moment and leave it at that. She was never quite the same though.

As the years went on we thinned out, as ya do, losing Mammy and Daddy along the way. It was hard for us all to say goodbye but they'd both reached a good age and sure, ya have t' go sometime. In fact, four of us have been laid t' rest as well now. Conor was first, just the fifty years he was, then there was Brigid, dear Brigid. Sean was next and, after a desperate few years with the dementia, poor Lizzy finally found peace. Oh, I'm wrong! Wee Roisin was the first we lost, of course she was - just a day old but our sister none the less. There's only Noel and Liam left now, over in England, then me and Maureen still here in the village. And haven't I been blessed with a fine smattering of nieces and nephews, with three of them over here? It's almost like having my own family, I see them that often.

'You can share them,' said Maureen, and never a truer word did I hear.

'Could I stay with you for a while, Aunty Carmel? Mammy and I have had a misunderstanding...' How many times did I hear that one!

I haven't missed out. No, not at all.

I love to crochet - made outfits for all the babies, I did. I have my bingo every week in the village hall and I do love my telly, especially the soaps. Wednesday night now, that's my favourite - two soaps and a crime thriller - it's just great, so it is. Of course, I love my books as well. I wouldn't want you t' think I'm in any way unsophisticated or deficient in the grey cells department either. I'll have you know I answer a good few questions on them there *"Eggheads"*. I can get quite excited, shouting at the telly. I only went and applied t' go on *"Who Wants To Be A Millionaire"*, I did! I'm still waiting to hear just now. Oh, how I'd love t' win a load of money to spread around the family. God knows, some of them need it. I'd probably treat myself to a few wee luxuries as well, though there's not a lot I want these days, and I manage quite well on what my pension gives me. Besides, too much money and ya might well be a target for them there "scammers" or "hackers" or whatever the crooks like t' call themselves these days. Trouble is, the more ya have, the more there is t' lose, and I can do without the extra worry.

I was thinking what a funny thing life is. If you're contented with your lot, they say you've no ambition. Sure, I gave up on "ambition" years ago and if it came knocking on my door now, I'd tell it t' clear off. Like Daddy used t' say, not everyone needs to be the General, foot soldiers are just as important. Well, I may have plodded my way through the years but I'm happy enough. Yes, I admit there are moments when I rail against lost love, and I still shed a tear for friends and family that are gone, but all in all I can't complain. Even if I did, sure there's no-one here t' listen.

***

You'll never believe what's after knocking on my door just now, and me thinking it was our Marie's youngest having a fall-out with her mother again. She's going through a difficult stage at the moment - "she" being my great niece. History repeating itself, so it is.

Anyways, I up and open the door while it's still in one piece, and I swear t' God I must have lost a couple of years off my life, the way my heart went into overdrive, for who should be standing right in front of me but Padraig himself. Still the lovely blue eyes, like crystals in a lake, so they are, smaller now of course as the auld wrinkles encroach - like they do - but still....

'How are ya Carmel?' says he, as bold as ya like.

When I manage t' get my breathing under control...

'Well, now Padraig,' says I, as if this was an everyday occurrence, *'You've not lost the accent, I see, considering the time that's passed since you were home'.*

It turned out he'd been widowed these three years and had decided to come back while he still had the strength left in his legs. He'd thought of me often, he said, over the years, and just wanted t' pay his respects before taking himself back home to his family. "Back home" - that said it all, didn't it?

***

So, I'll just go on sitting here in the warmth of my beloved house, staring at the flames dancing on the hearth, and take comfort that he's still fighting fit. I take comfort too, that he lit my flame again, if only for a moment. Ah, but what a moment!

Sure it makes ya feel alive, so it does.

MUCH ADO ABOUT NOTHING

Tony Rattigan

Paris 1880

The poet sat at the table in his lonely garret and tried to write poetry. Once again the blank page stared back at him, mocking him, daring him to write something other than the usual dull, trite, useless verbiage that he normally produced.

The room was humid as the rain fell over Paris. Not a monsoon-like downpour that would clear the air but a steady drizzle that only seemed to raise the temperature. He got out of his chair and went and opened the French windows. (Well, what else would they be, in Paris?) They opened out onto a small balcony. When it wasn't raining, from here high in his garret in the hilly, Montmartre district, he could see across "The City of Lights", as far as the Eiffel Tower.

The poet was English but when he came to live in Paris he decided to live in Montmartre amongst the other artists, writers and poets. For it was his life-long ambition to be a famous poet, a goal he felt, that would he would surely achieve one day. Here he truly felt at home amongst his fellow, impoverished artists.

Like them he lived in the poorest part of the quarter and lived on a diet of mainly cigarettes and wine, occasionally supplemented by bread, cheese and cabbage soup, courtesy of his landlady. (Although, truth be told, he came from a middle-class, fairly well-to-do family, who regularly sent money to his local bank. The poet however believed that to truly produce great works, one must suffer for your art. Therefore, he confined himself to only drawing a hundred Francs a month from the bank.)

He got a small, shot-glass from the cupboard, put it in a larger, empty glass and then filled the shot-glass with Absinthe – The Green Lady, as it was also known. Then he poured cold water into the shot glass until the Absinthe overflowed into the bigger glass, creating the milky blend or *louche* as it is called. Finally he stirred in a spoonful of sugar. Absinthe was powerful stuff but tonight was no night for wine; he needed something stronger to cope with his mood.

Sitting back down at his table, he lit a cigarette. He smoked around sixty Gauloises a day in the hope that it would give him a consumption-like cough, but so far his chest had remained disappointingly clear of phlegm.

The poet longed with all his heart for his poetry to be appreciated, praised by his peers, lauded by the masses and sold out in print. He wanted to be revered and make his fortune. Alas, his works so far only aroused scorn from the various publishers and newspaper editors that he sent his work to. He even got booed on 'Open Poetry' nights in the local bars. That hurt the most. They were his own kind with whom he shared the deprivations of this artistic ghetto; surely they should have been more understanding. His work was prolific to be sure, he wrote copious amounts of poetry, but he never seemed to hit upon that *one special poem* that would win everyone over and make them re-evaluate the rest of his work.

He sipped his Absinthe. Picking up his quill he dipped it into the ink and his hand hovered over the empty page. Five minutes later he cursed and scrubbed out the mouse that he had been doodling. He prepared another glass of Absinthe and lit another cigarette.

'Damn it, why can't I write a good poem?' he cried out to the room.

'Perhaps because you try too hard,' came the reply.

The poet started, nearly spilling his drink. 'Who's there? How did you get in?'

A man stepped forward from the shadows cast by the oil lamp. 'Calm yourself, you need have no fear of me. I am a friend come to aid you.'

Looking him up and down the poet was puzzled. The man looked all wrong. He had a high, starched collar around his neck and he wore knee-breeches. The stranger had a high forehead (which was a polite way of saying he was going bald) and a moustache and beard. The poet was on the point of raising the alarm when it struck him that the man looked familiar.

'You look just like … you're not are you? Are you William Shakespeare?'

'Indeed I am.'

'But you're dead.'

'Alas, I am that also.'

'Oh my God, I've had too much Absinthe. They say it sometimes makes you hallucinate.'

'Maybe that is true but in this instance it's not the case. What you see before you is real, I am real. I am Will Shakespeare's ghost, at your service.'

There was a long pause and then the poet asked, 'Why are you here? Why have you appeared to me? I'm not dead, am I?'

'No, no, nothing at all like that. I have come to you because I heard the cry from the soul of another poet, another *Englishman* and I could not deny that heart-felt plea for assistance. So I came. I understand you are troubled because no one will recognise your talent or appreciate your work.'

The poet was about to bluster when he realised the

futility of lying to a ghost.

'Yes, you're right. Nobody likes my work, I can't get published, and I'm destined to remain in obscurity.'

'Allow me to let you in on a little secret. Were it not for the fact that I part owned the acting company known as "The Lord Chamberlain's Men", I too might have remained in obscurity. As it was, I could present my own work to the company, to save them money on buying plays.'

'But you're the most famous playwright of all time.'

'I am now,' agreed Shakespeare, 'but back then I was a nobody until I bought my way into the company. If I've learnt one thing over the years it's that success is no measure of talent. Take Arthur Penworthy for example.'

'Who?'

'Exactly. One of the finest poets and lyricists you'll ever meet. Died penniless and obscure in a Whitehall brothel. *And boy does he go on about it.* But my point is that he kept trying in the face of constant failure, right up until his death. You must do the same.'

'But it's hard, living in poverty, facing constant rejection, I don't know if I have it in me anymore.'

'Nonsense, as long as you can choose some pretty words and make each line scan, you can do it. You don't even have to make them rhyme!'

The poet shook his head. 'I have such grand ideas for my poems but I can't force the words to do my bidding. I try and bend them into what I want to say but it never works.'

'And *that* is where you go wrong. You confuse form with function. You shouldn't try and twist the words to your meaning; rather you should feel the emotions in your soul, bring out the truth of your heart's reasoning and once you have that, then choose the words that properly explain the virtues of your intent. *You are a*

Wordsmith. As a blacksmith takes the raw iron and transforms it into a desired shape or form, you must take the raw material – the letters of the alphabet – and mould them into such words as would make the angels weep with delight. If such words or phrases do not exist, then make them up as I did.'

'You made up your own words?'

'Certainly I did. Words such as "Dauntless", "Lackluster", "Dwindle" and many others. Although actually I'm more famous for the phrases I invented, "Dead as a doornail", "All of a sudden", "The green-eyed monster", "Just one of those things",' he paused, 'or was that Cole Porter? I can never remember. No matter, there are plenty of other examples I could give but that's neither here nor there, right now.'

'Who's Cole Porter?' asked the poet.

'Never mind about that now, it's not important.'

'So you, the greatest poet the world has ever known, are telling me that I should keep on writing poetry and one day it will be recognised?'

'Exactly.'

'Then with that encouragement I shall plough on.'

'I have said my piece and now I shall withdraw, to let you ponder on what I have said.' Shakespeare retreated into the shadows but before he faded away completely he told the poet, 'Remember, listen to your heart and your soul, they will provide the meaning you seek, then it is your job to translate that into words.' With that, he was gone.

The poet poured himself another drink and sat quietly smoking, thinking through the night's events. Had it been real or just a figment of his imagination? It didn't really matter he concluded, the message was clear. Write and keep writing until you make the breakthrough, until you master the art, until you release that *one great poem* that he had inside him.

Filling up his glass again he set to work. He wrote and rewrote, accepting then discarding idea after idea, throwing the rejected pieces carelessly on the floor. Drinking and smoking, his head full of Absinthe, rhymes and ghosts, he scribbled away into the night.

***

Next morning

The poet slowly, painfully, opened his eyes. The pillow was wet where he had drooled onto it. As he sat up, an action which he immediately regretted, his foot hit the glass, which rolled across the floor and 'clinked' into the empty Absinthe bottle. He looked at it. *That was nearly full when I started on it*, he thought.

What happened last night? How much of it was drink inspired flights of fancy? Had he really talked to the ghost of the Bard of Avon? At the moment it was all too hazy, so he put it aside, to be examined later.

The downpour had stopped and the sun had come up. The rooftops steamed gently as the morning sun evaporated the night's rain. He managed to get to his feet and by gingerly 'walking' his way along the wall with his hands, made it to the sink where he splashed water on his face and then drank several glasses of it. God he felt rough. He knew from experience that Absinthe gave the worst headaches. It would be one of *those* hangovers – one of those where at first you're afraid you're going to die. Then later, you're afraid that you're *not* going to.

He gazed around the room, the floor was littered with screwed up pieces of paper. Obviously his poor, misguided attempts to write a masterpiece, each rejected and discarded in the moment of its creation. *All is failure*, he thought. Then he froze, with the glass of water halfway to his mouth.

There on the table in the centre of the room, was a sheet of paper, lying between the quill and the half-empty ink bottle. He could see from this distance that there was writing on it. His heart began to pound in his chest. Could this be it? It hadn't been thrown away like the other attempts and he had left it in a prominent place, so that he would see it when he woke.

The end of the night, when he'd gone to bed, was a total blank. Had he at last ceased his frantic scribblings because he had accomplished his task, or was it simply fatigue? Had he taken the ghost's advice and finally created the masterpiece that would cause him to be remembered, down through the ages? The poem that would put him up there with Keats, Byron, Tennyson and, dare he say it, Shakespeare himself?

He put down his glass of water, walked unsteadily to the table and sat in the chair, his eyes deliberately avoiding the writing on the paper. He didn't want to catch a glance of part of it by accident; he wanted to take in the full effect of his creation, as it was intended, line by line.

Although his head was pounding from the Absinthe and his heart was about to burst from his chest with anticipation, he forced himself to sit calmly for a moment and look straight ahead, avoiding sight of the page.

Eventually he leaned forward and rested his elbows on the table, allowing his eyes to drop to the page. He read the poem, then he read it again, slowly, analysing it a line at a time. He had written it in capital letters so that he wouldn't ruin it with his drunken, spidery scrawl.

Finally, after all the months of frustration, it had come to this. Something inside him snapped, at first it was just a heartfelt sob, then after resting his head in his hands, the dam broke and the tears came flooding out like rain.

He cried for several minutes and then wordlessly he got out of the chair, walked to the open window and threw himself over the balcony, to crash onto the street below. As luck would have it, a couple of gendarmes were making their rounds when they saw the young man throw himself to his death.

With cries of 'Mon Dieu' and 'Sacre Bleu' they dashed over to his broken body but the way his head had split open and his blood ran in rivulets among the wet cobbles, told them that it was far too late to render assistance. They entered the lodging house and made their way up to the garret. Drawing their pistols in case there was an assailant inside, they entered the room. Once they had established that the room was empty, they holstered their weapons and began a more detailed inspection. Despite the untidiness and the paper scattered across the floor, there were no signs of a struggle, so that seemed to rule out foul play. They looked at each other and one of them gave "the Gallic shrug".

One of them approached the table and mindful of his superior's constant reminders not to disturb the scene of a crime, merely leaned over to read the page instead of picking it up. Perhaps it was a suicide note. Unfortunately, he did not have 'le Anglaise' so he called his colleague over who did, to read it.

The second gendarme read the poem, his lips moving silently as he did. His partner motioned for him to read it out aloud, so he complied:

'THERE WAS A YOUNG MAN FROM NANTUCKET ...'

REST HOME RHYTHM AND BLUES

Sue Tompkinson

Please take my hand so I can make
my way across this pristine floor
of pungent pine and non-slip shine
to reach that comfy chair.

Please hold me safe, my slippered feet
can only shuffle to the beat
of slip-slip-go and stop-stop-slow,
that *"Strictly"* would despair.

Please hold me soft, don't tear my skin,
so fragile now, so pale, so thin.
The merest touch can mark or bruise
complexion, once so fair.

Ah, once so fair and beautiful
or so you told me when you held
me warm and safe in sweet caress
when life was young and free.

I loved the way you took my hand
and nothing marred such happiness,
to taint or spoil or cause distress.
Your eyes fell soft on me.

And still you're here, with wrinkled brow,
your body bent, no longer lithe
and handsome features hidden well
beneath time's raging sea.

Please take my hand, escape with me,
we two old spouses, giggling now,
to where love's wild and reckless still.
Well, later - after tea.

TRANSGRESSION

Chris Allen

"I have seen you as you watch with ancient eyes and leaf beard face. Are you spirit of emerald wood and deep, dark forest or merely born a thing of tavern signs, hung to tempt? Some say you are no more than this but I know otherwise. From the day of my birth, my soul has known you are waiting, silent and inscrutable, though we have not yet met and never may."

Richie awakes with a start, the words of the dream still echoing in the recesses of his mind. He feels the cool softness of grass against his cheek and manages to force open his eyes, blinking to clear lids that feel gummed together.

Before him is the dim shape of a timber bench leg. He groans and, with a herculean effort, rolls clumsily over onto his back. The sky revolves, steadies and then comes into focus.

Above him stars blaze with ice-blue fire across a sable backcloth, scattered like tossed diamonds in the night.

Another roll, and Richie is on all fours with his head hanging down. His right hand is wet; he looks down and sees a small pool of vomit oozing between his fingers. The sharp odour rises to his nostrils and, as realisation hits him, his stomach performs a slow, greasy somersault. Stifling nausea and the urge to gag, he somehow finds the strength to sit up and back onto his knees. He looks groggily around, trying to take stock of his surroundings. The world is bright with moonlight and in the pale light, he sees that he is kneeling in the garden of a pub. Around him the tables and benches stand like sentinels, and all is silent; no rustle of trees in the breeze that strokes his face softly like a caress, no sharp animal movement from the hedges that form the boundary between garden and the farmland beyond.

The pub itself crouches by the road, unlit windows forming harsh, black rectangles that stand out in contrast against the white, half-timbered walls. By the car park, a deserted rectangle of gravel, he can see a sign pasted askew on a sandwich noticeboard. Weirdly, despite the distance, Richie finds he can read the words which say "Party this Midsummer at the Green Man! Celebrate the solstice with us! Happy Hour 'til 8:00 pm."

The sign trips a switch in his head and, slowly, slowly, memory rises like bubble of oil in water. He was here with Bez and Gary and, by the way and come to think of it, where exactly the fuck are they, anyway? Some mates they are, leaving him like this! Richie is gradually starting to feel a bit more human. Bracing himself against the table, he lurches to his feet, still swaying slightly. His mouth is dry and thick with the stale taste of alcohol and puke. Jesus, he thinks, exactly how much did he drink? He attempts to spit, to clear his mouth, but only succeeds in producing a string of glutinous bile that drips down his chin and hangs suspended in the air. Swearing under his breath, he wipes his face with the back of his hand and looks around him again.

The night is still silent, the car park still deserted, and the pub still crouches furtively at the side of the road.

A hard knot of apprehension forms in Richie's gut and he suddenly, desperately, wishes that he could see someone, anyone else. He walks towards the pub, looking up at the sign that bears its name and another recollection snaps into his consciousness of himself, Gary and that idiot Bez singing a drunken song with a refrain that went something like "Green Man, Green Man, what a little twat…" For no apparent reason, he shivers.

Time to go home, he decides and lurches stiffly forwards. His home is three miles distant down the country lanes. It will be a long, slow journey on foot he thinks sourly. Passing by the entrance to the pub, he looks up once again at the sign, but the Green Man does not return his gaze. Richie walks to the road, turns left, and disappears from view.

Minutes pass. The world is frozen into immobility. As if at a signal the air thickens and ripples. Underneath the sign something stands where, moments before, there was nothing, a green-black figure with shaggy, foliate head and limbs. It pauses and the head moves from side to side in a motion curiously reminiscent of a snake tasting the air. Suddenly alert, it moves forward with swift, fluid paces, reaches the road and, turning left, disappears from view.

NO, THAT'S SPELT G-U-I-D-O

Tony Rattigan

Location: A custody suite, in a London nick.

Time: The early hours of 5th November 1605.

'So,' said the custody sergeant, licking the nib of his quill as he looked down at the forlorn individual being gripped tightly by two constables, 'Last name?'

'Fawkes,' came the reply.

'That would be ... F-O-R-K-S?'

'No, that would be F-A-W-K-E-S.'

'First name?'

'Guido.'

There was a pause while the sergeant thought about this. 'And that's G-E-E-D-O?'

'Wrong, it's spelt G-U-I-D-O.'

The sergeant mouthed it silently a few times and then commented, 'But surely that would be pronounced GUIDE-O, as in Travel Guide, Forest Guide ... Girl Guide?'

'Oh forget it, just call me, Guy!' said the prisoner, in exasperation.

'"Guy" it is then,' said the sergeant, writing it down with a satisfied air. He didn't like anomalies in his charge book, particularly as he would be the one who had to explain them to the inspector.

'Now then, what's he charged with?'

The younger of the two constables piped up, 'He was protesting outside the Houses of Parliament.'

'Protesting how?'

'He was marching up and down carrying this placard,' the constable held up the sign which read:

DOWN WITH THE PROTESTANT GOVERNMENT! BRING BACK THE CATHOLICS!

'Is that all?' asked the sergeant.

'He was also shouting "Down with King James", that's got to be treasonous, ain't it Sarge?'

'Maybe so constable, but can you prove it? Have you got any witnesses? Things aren't as easy as when I was a young copper. It's all well and good beating a confession out of a suspect but they've got this new-fangled thing they demand nowadays. What do they call it? Providence? Dividends? *Evidence!* Evidence, that's it. Dead hot on it now they are, won't let you execute anyone without it. That's modern policing for you. The world's gone to pot if you ask me,' he said, shaking his head.

'But we've got the sign!'

'Yes, well ... "Down with the Protestant government", "Bring back the Catholics" ... there are those that would say these are entirely reasonable points of view and as an Englishman he's entitled to speak his mind.'

The young constable's face dropped. This would have been his first arrest and Mum would have been *so proud*.

Feeling sorry for the constable and trying to help him out, he turned to the prisoner and asked, 'And what have you got to say for yourself, Mr. "I-can't-even-spell-my-own-name-right" Fawkes. Was you saying, "Down with the King"?'

'Yes, yes I was. I not only admit, I'm proud of it,' he answered excitedly. 'Note today's date well, Sergeant, for today marks the beginning of the glorious, people's revolution. I was chosen by my colleagues to bring the revolution to the attention of the people. My intent was to stand proudly in front of the Houses of Parliament and cry out to the world, "Arise good Catholic people and throw off your Protestant chains! Let the Protestant King know that we will suffer his rule no longer!" And then the people would rush out onto the streets and gather together and be drawn to Parliament by the sound of my voice and together we would overthrow our wicked rulers.

'Oh, I tell you Sergeant, this night will go down in history and all around the Catholic world I shall be proclaimed a hero, as the leader of the revolution. I was even chosen because they thought that *my name* was the most suitable to be the one that lives on, and even this night will be named after me and remembered for evermore ... Guy Fawkes Night.'

'And who chose you?'

'My friends, Bertie Bonfire and Freddie Firework.'

There was a long pause while everyone thought this through, then the older constable sidled over to the sergeant and muttered quietly in his ear, 'Look Sarge, what about all that gunpowder they found under the Houses of Parliament? Can't we fit him up with that somehow?'

'That's not a bad idea.'

'Trouble is we've got no whatchamacallit, evidence,' the constable pointed out.

'Leave it to me,' replied the sergeant. He took his pipe out and began patting his pockets. 'Anyone got a light?'

he asked innocently.

The two constables looked at each other and the older one shook his head slightly, so they both stood there with vacant looks on their faces.

Finally, Guy Fawkes went, 'Tch, here,' and threw a box of matches to the sergeant.

'There you go,' said the sergeant, holding up the box of matches, 'evidence! Proof that he has the ability to set fire to the gunpowder underneath the Houses of Parliament. He has the means, the motive and the opportunity to blow them all up.'

'*Gunpowder?*' said the dismayed Fawkes. 'What gunpowder?'

'Guilty as charged,' said the sergeant. 'Haul him off and burn him. I'll get the judge to pronounce him guilty in the morning.'

'Can't we just hang him, Sarge?'

'But we always burn Catholics.'

'Yes but it takes ages to collect the wood for a burning,' complained the young copper. 'We'll be here all night doing that and we should be out on patrol again.'

'Oh, very well then,' sighed the sergeant, wishing he didn't have to keep in with the boy's mother, but she did do a lovely Steak and Kidney pie. 'A hanging it is, but be quick about it, like you say, you're meant to be out on patrol.'

The two constables disappeared out of view, dragging the unfortunate Fawkes with them, who was still proclaiming, 'What gunpowder? I don't know anything about any bloody gunpowder. I demand to see my lawyer!'

The sergeant misused the evidence to light his pipe and then settled down to read his paper. *Bloody revolutionaries. Who needs 'em,* he thought. *That one will disappear into history and never be heard of again.*

THE COMMUTE

Mark Fletcher

Hatchley-Meadow Lane was anything but small, the road was over two miles long, and would boast some of the town's largest and most extravagant houses. The people who resided in such lavish abodes were those who were regarded as 'high earners', doctors, lawyers, and maybe the odd company director or manager.

Ryan lived on the Hillman council estate on the other side of town, four miles and a world away. Yet he would drive through Hatchley-Meadow Lane every weekday on his commute to work. Some would've called it 'taking the scenic route', but for Ryan it was merely a 'means to an end'. This vast and extravagant highway merely served as the quickest route to work, and any scenery viewed upon the way would just be a painful reminder of what he would never have. It wasn't just a lack of wealth that made Ryan resent the area either, his father had rarely had anything good to say about the area from his days of being a postman.

"It takes you five minutes to walk up each drive, yet you end up taking ten, because you do anything that resembles a short-cut and they're onto the depot!" he would moan.

Ryan's only interaction with the residents, had been when he turned his car around on the grass verge outside of someone's driveway, just to be met by an eloquent speaking - albeit hysterical, lady armed with a spiked umbrella, "How dare you!" she had screamed. Apart from that his only other altercation was with Mr Charles, one of the directors at the factory where he worked. Like most people on the shop floor, Ryan found Mr Charles nothing more than a pompous, arrogant 'mini-Hitler', and probably the person who set the bar highest for his father's personal summary of the road's residents.

The temporary traffic lights had caused the traffic to move slower than normal down the main road. Ryan's old Fiesta clunked and groaned noisily as he went through the gears, causing a middle aged lady, walking her well-groomed poodle alongside him, to become startled, before frowning and walking off hurriedly.

"Posh cow," Ryan said aloud. He stared out at some of the houses as his car trundled along, all detached, and all unique. One house had a thatched roof, another must have had thirty windows at the front, and another had a water feature in the middle of its garden that was bigger than the one belonging to Opal Shopping Centre in town. Ryan noted in his head the makes of the cars parked on the driveways. Jaguars, Porsches, Bentleys.

'They're probably all up in arms over the road being dug up,' he thought to himself, 'every cloud.'

Ryan was just about to put his car into third gear when he spotted him. There, standing in his grey suit, was Mr Charles, at a bus stop no less! Ryan looked at him puzzlingly, the works manager looked red-faced as he stood there in the drizzle, briefcase in one hand and a golfing umbrella in the other. A devilish thought went through Ryan's head, to drive through the biggest puddle in range, in order to drench him. After all, Mr Charles hadn't even noticed him, and why would he? He didn't notice him on the shop floor or anyone else below him, unless of course he had a bee in his bonnet, in which case no one was safe, and innocence was irrelevant. Ryan smiled to himself, "No, I'm the better man and I'll show him," he told himself. He pulled his car alongside Mr

Charles, leaning over to open the passenger, in his most deliberate false voice; "Good morning Mr Charles, would one care for a lift to one's place of work??"

Mr Charles was still frowning as he looked into Ryan's car, whether it was because he had taken offence by Ryan's smugness, or that it was because he was contemplating on whether or not to lower himself to getting into his car. Arriving to work in the factory labourer's second hand car? Oh the shame.

Mr Charles looked back towards the main road, the bus was still nowhere to be seen, he thought for a few seconds before Ryan piped up again; "Make your mind up, Sir, I'll be getting docked 15 minutes pay otherwise", he tried to display a balance of both seriousness and jest on his facial expression as he did. Mr Charles meanwhile was trying to negotiate a balance of both supremacy and gratitude on his own demeanour.

"Err, yes ok then," he said, as he shuffled awkwardly into Ryan's car, before adding, "Thank you." Ryan waited for him to close the door before setting off again.

Ryan's car had barely moved twenty yards before he decided to speak up. In the past, he had yet to share constructive dialogue with his manager, but with the car absent of its radio, he felt that a silent commute whilst sitting next to one other would surely manifest into a new level of awkwardness; "So, dare I ask where the Rolls Royce is?" enquired Ryan,

"I've got a flat," his manager bluntly replied, "and the recovery vehicle can't come out for at least an hour, and the taxi companies weren't much use either," he grumbled.

"A flat??" Ryan replied, in disbelief, trying not to laugh.

"Yes, a flat, as in - a flat tyre," Mr Charles replied indignantly,

"Well I didn't think you meant as in a place where say, I would live," Ryan curtly replied, "I mean, they're easy enough to change, no need for the AA, say."

Mr Charles looked slightly embarrassed as they passed his house, partly because of his inability to change a tyre, and partly because his thinking that Ryan would be envious of his house. Ryan glanced over. It was common knowledge on the shop floor that Mr Charles lived on this road, but he never knew which house it was precisely, but with the Rolls Royce parked on the driveway with 'CHARLES1' emblazoned on the licence plate, it was now quite obvious. Ryan tried to look like he didn't care but it was hard not to. The redbrick wall around the house was about 4ft high, black metal railings continued upwards from it. Mr Charles' Rolls Royce looked quite lonely, given the amount of space his frontage provided. It was entirely block-paved, aside from a few purpose built flower beds, boasting a few immaculate rose bushes. The house itself looked like a red brick stately home, a large oak door sat between two large windows on either side, with five windows sat perfectly above, one above the front door, the other two above their respective downstairs window. Ryan tried to look as disinterested as possible but couldn't help but ask about his mansion;

"So how many rooms do you have?"

"Seven," replied Mr Charles sheepishly.

"Bloody hell, that's a lot to hoover" replied Ryan, masking his envy, Mr Charles chose not to reply about employing a cleaner.

"So, what did the taxis say earlier?" Ryan asked offhandedly as they turned onto a modern council estate, the new builds barely five years old.

"Nothing this way for at least an hour, bloody disgrace, I would've came in later but we've got the Americans in today for a big visit, so as you know, everything has to be pristine."

'Bloody hell, remind me I'm just the labourer,' thought Ryan, "Goes without saying Mr Charles," replied Ryan in automated fashion, only half masking his sarcasm.

"Well so long as you know, and I do appreciate you picking me up, I can't say I was looking forward to getting the bus," although Ryan's opinion on public transport wasn't exactly complimentary he wasn't ready to yet agree with Mr Charles' take on it. Ryan pulled over outside a small communal block of flats, talking as he did.

"Yeah you don't want to be sharing a bus with the riff-raff, right I'll be back in a minute, if you want the window down then I'm afraid that the war machine doesn't have electric windows, so you might want to roll your arm up," Ryan winked as he closed the car door and headed into the flats, leaving a bemused Mr Charles waiting on him.

Less than a couple of minutes later Ryan emerged from the flats with a young boy, no older that thirteen, in school uniform. He opened the door and moved his seat forward, allowing the boy to climb in. Ryan sat in the driver's seat and turned to face both the boy and Mr Charles; "Mr Charles, this is my son Toby. Toby, this is my boss, Mr Charles."

Mr Charles turned to greet Toby, and was quite taken aback when Toby put his hand out to shake his. Throughout the rest of the journey Mr Charles asked Toby various questions about his age, his school, and other trivial pursuits, to a point where now it was Ryan who was feeling uncomfortable.

Before long they pulled up outside the Toll Cross Secondary School, a large school situated a few streets away from the factory, Ryan turned to face him; "Right son, your mum has told me that she's had a word with the school, and those kids have been told, but well done on your test, keep that up son, then one day you can live in a big house like Mr Charles here." Ryan went to get out and move his seat forward, but surprisingly Mr Charles had opted to get out and do the same,

"It's ok, I'll do it, the paths on my side after all."

Toby said goodbye to his father, before getting out and saying goodbye to Mr Charles; "Nice to meet you Mr Charles," he said, before walking through the school gates, Mr Charles sat back in the car,

"He's a very polite young man,", he commented.

Ryan frowned, "Of course he is, I didn't raise a feral," he replied, rather defiantly.

The remainder of the journey was short, and little was said until they came in through the work's main gates, Mr Charles had felt like he had maybe offended the very person who had gave him a lift, whereas Ryan was now thinking that he had maybe overstepped the mark. Ryan cleared his throat, as he decided to speak first; "So, are you doing much other the weekend?"

"My youngest has her horse-riding class on Saturday, but on Sunday I'm off to play golf," he replied,

"Golf? Where do you play?" Ryan asked, pretending to show an interest.

"Oakwell," replied Mr Charles, before adding, "Do you know it?"

"No, but whatever your handicap I'm sure you'd come unstuck against me if we played ... on my preferred course that is."

"Really?" Mr Charles asked, taken aback by the challenge, "Where?"

"Buccaneer's Cove, right on Penmouth seafront!"

Both men laughed as they pulled up outside the main doors.

"Well thank you for this, I do appreciate it," said Mr Charles sincerely.

"No problem," Ryan shrugged, "I'm sure you would've done it for me," he added. Mr Charles again looked sheepish as he got out the car before Ryan asked him, "I don't suppose I could have your parking space could I? I would get out a hell of lot quicker come the end of the day."

Mr Charles went to nervously reply before Ryan cut back in, "It's ok, I'm just kidding," before driving off down the far end of the carpark.

A TRANQUIL SEA

June Bradley

He parked the car at the top of the beach, put on the handbrake and sat back in his seat.

"Last chance," he said softly turning to look at her, "Are you sure about this?"

She looked at him and smiled, one of her smiles that told him, 'Just let me get on with it please'.

The incoming tide was quite calm. No frothing of petulant petticoats of foam racing to hit the beach first, unlike last night, just a steady inevitable advancement of an unbreakable cycle. He switched off the engine and got out of the car then walked around to the passenger door and opened it for her.

"Here let me take those," he offered.

She passed him the backpack and her memory foam cushion and eased herself out of the seat. They had carried out a dummy run the night before although the sea was much rougher than tonight and there had been a buffeting wind.

"Better tonight," he stated, as they both donned head torches. "Have you got your 'phone?" She nodded making the beam dance up and down. "And your whistle for emergencies?"

"Yes love, just as we practised last night. I'll be fine and you'll only be a few yards away from me."

"Sorry, I worry about you Lizzie."

"I know, but I'll be fine. It will be closure for all of us." She touched his face with her fingertips. "Let's go, it's nearly time."

He hefted the backpack onto his shoulders and tucked the cushion under one arm. She heard the familiar clunk of central locking as they turned and walked hand in hand across the top of the beach, torch lights bobbing in unison, to the long peninsular rock at the far side. She remembered less of an incline on the approaching slope to the top and was surprised last night at how her leg muscles pulled and how sore they were now, but then it had been almost forty years since she'd trod this particular path. When they reached the top he walked with her almost to the end.

"This will do," she said.

He placed the cushion to her desired position and steadied her as she lowered herself onto it. She looked up at him.

"Succour for an ageing spine eh?"

"Just be careful when you stand up please love, blow the whistle if…"

"I will. Now don't fuss, just let me get on with it," she said, shooing him away.

He put the backpack down beside her and turned to go.

"Remember," he said quietly, "I'm just …"

"At the bottom of the slope, I know. It won't take too long." She pulled the small Thermos flask from the side pocket of the bag and handed it to him. "Here, take a hot drink, don't let yourself get cold."

He took it from her and set off down the slope.

"Use the whistle if you need me," he called then disappeared out of sight.

She turned back to face the sea. Wriggling for a more comfortable position she drew up her legs and hugged her knees. There was a stronger breeze here with a nip to the air but her padded jacket was doing a good job and she was quite comfortable. She turned off her head torch and watched the slivers of gold ooze slowly across the horizon. As the minutes passed, an ingress of colour began to wash the sky flooding the purple black of night, gradually engorging it with sunlight. Amber, pink and lavender slowly replaced the dark tones, until there was only daylight. Nature's watercolour masterpiece never failed to move her. She unzipped her jacket as the chill began to lift and wondered if she had been right to agree this.

"Strange isn't it, Mo?" she began. "Being back on this beach? Our beach we called it." She paused and continued, "I've never had the urge to return. The first few years it was too painful and you would always be with me like it or not."

She shifted slightly, easing her shoulders back.

"The first time I saw you was the summer of 1981, all muscles, white teeth and sun gold hair. You had a ready smile and a fingertip caress of the hand for all the girls who gathered around the surf centre on the main beach. Word of a new instructor swept around the town quicker than a verruca outbreak at the local swimming baths and I tagged along with my friend Trudie for a glimpse of the new 'Adonis' out of interest. Yes, I admit it, you were worth the investigation but you were almost twice our age and the competition was much too fierce. Besides, Mum and Dad kept the apron strings pretty taut and I was studying for exams to get into the sixth form at school and hopefully onto university. I worked Saturdays at the beach café and served you quite regularly. You always thanked me but it was a kid sister appreciation and at the end of the summer your parting shot as you finished your sandwich was 'See you next year kiddo, your braces should be off by then.' You laughed, waved and blew me a kiss and I wore the blush for the rest of the day. The manager at the surf centre told me, under my badly disguised interrogation that you worked in sales out of season, sometimes double glazing, sometimes timeshare."

She smiled, remembering her fathers' immediate summing up when he heard that particular snippet of information. "Peter Pan in a pinstripe suit, overgrown beach bum led through life by his…"

I remember my Mum stopping the flow with, "Yes, thank you very much, Bill, we get the drift!" Then he looked me straight in the eye and warned, "Don't even think about it young lady!"

"Pretty accurate wasn't he?" she whispered.

"Sorry, this is taking longer than I planned but you need to hear all this. You owe me that much at least."

She looked at the sea. It wore a golden sheen as the sun rose further and further from the horizon.

"Anyway," she continued, "the following year not only had I acquired straight teeth, but also a 36B bra, cheekbones and several acceptances from various universities of my choice pending results. You didn't quite believe it was me did you? I think you only asked to meet me for confirmation. But by then I was in awe of you. Trudie warned me to be careful, that you'd been seen around with numerous other girls but I ignored her, even accused her of being jealous and used her as an excuse to my parents so that you and I could meet on this beach. You introduced me to the music of Eric Clapton and we'd listen to Derek and the Dominoes 'Layla' over and over on your cassette player while the setting sun warmed our bodies. Some evenings you didn't turn up, but it would only make my appetite stronger for you the next time we met; clever tactic, Mo, you knew all the tricks didn't you? But I have to concede, you never actually told me that you loved me. You whispered that I deserved to be loved, that I was special and refreshing; you even said that I made you happy. But you were careful to never actually commit to the 'L' word.

"By the beginning of September I knew and when I saw you that heavy overcast lunchtime and said I had something to tell you, your gaze moved to the horizon and back to the sand at your feet. When you lifted your head you couldn't meet my gaze. 'Meet me tonight on our beach' you whispered, then you turned and walked away. I never saw or heard from you again. But that was your thing wasn't it? Run away, love them and leave them. You wore responsibility and commitment like an ill-fitting jacket. When the time came for you to straighten up and grasp the lapels the stitches unravelled, it fell from your shoulders and you slipped from our lives without a word.

"When I didn't come home Mum and Dad asked Trudie if she knew where I could be. They found me here, took me home and Trudie stayed for the rest of the week, tissues in one hand, dry toast in the other. My best friend, we still see each other when work and family commitments allow.

"When the baby was born I called her Layla.

"For a long time I hated you, but eventually realised I was wasting energy that could be put to better use. Mum and Dad helped with the baby, I continued my studies and got a place at university again. We all moved nearer to Nottingham so that I could, with help, still be a mum to Layla. I did pretty well, got a decent job and an old banger of a car. Layla was six when I met Geoff. He fixed my car and slowly repaired my heart. He's the best thing that ever happened to me and I trust him with my life."

She paused for a moment.

"She's thirty eight now, and believe me when I say your life was so much the poorer for not being part of hers. She lives in Australia with her husband and two sons. The older one wants to be a software designer like his dad, the younger, well, he has sun gold hair and swims like a fish so we'll just wait and see. Geoff and I have a son, who with his wife have just made us grandparents again.

"I suspect this is all far too domestic and cosy for you Mo, but each to his own eh? By the way, I'm still a big Eric Clapton fan, but I much prefer the ninety two unplugged version of 'Layla' that Geoff and I have in our collection."

Lizzie shifted position again, straightened and pushed her shoulders back once more. She noticed how calm the sea had become. The tide had peaked and was gently lapping against the base of the rock waiting for a signal to begin its ebb. She settled herself and looked up into an unblemished cerulean sky.

"The solicitor's letter was a bit of a surprise," she said quietly. "I checked him out before getting in touch of course; you can't be too careful nowadays, but it seems everything was legal and above board. Layla is going to put the legacy in 'Trust' for the boys and says understandably that she doesn't want any of it. I'm amazed quite honestly at you having property of any sort and even more surprised at a six bedroom villa. But the Virgin Islands? Well that's right up your street."

She shook her head and smiled.

"But why me? Was I the only person throughout your life who you could trust? Your previous partners were all less than gracious at what they would like to do with you apparently; none of the suggestions appropriate to a peaceful afterlife I might add. The solicitor said that he would understand if I preferred not to, but I was a specific request. I'm not a cruel person Mo, acting out of spite won't change the past."

She inhaled deeply and watched a flock of seagulls out at sea, their calls raucous and urgent searching for food.

"Strangely enough, I wasn't surprised when he told me the circumstances. An afternoon business meeting with a lady client in an exclusive hotel … Oh really? … You'd just left her suite heading for the main entrance and … Wham!" Lizzie clicked her fingers. "You were dead before you hit the floor, massive coronary, he said."

She sat quietly for a while. The tide had turned. A bank of cloud was forming inland. With the help of a sharp breeze; that blew her hair around her face and into her eyes, it was heading towards the sea. She tucked the fretful strands behind her ears and zipped up her jacket, pulling the collar close around her neck, then reached across and opened the backpack. Inside were a small box and a larger bag, which could have held enough salt to thaw the icy paths around her garden and front steps on a wintry day. But it didn't. It had been coloured with vegetable dyes to mimic the shades of the sea and it sat on a folded raffia bag exactly as the solicitors letter of instructions had said. She lifted out the box and removed the lid.

"Such a lack of pomp for such a colourful life," she said softly, touching the contents with the pad of her forefinger. It was like fine sand, the colour of a tropical beach. "Very fitting," she whispered.

The breeze whipped at her hair again as she watched foaming crests form on the retreating waves. She shifted onto her knees and stood up cautiously, then held the box out as far as she could and slowly tipped it forward. It trickled slowly at first, disappearing below the rock onto the fractious water, then as it gained momentum the breeze whipped it upwards in a display of passionate swirling and twisting until it was snatched away by the turbulence, dissipating into the sky. She turned back and placed the PVA bag and the empty box inside the raffia bag and tied the loop handles together. She prayed that it wouldn't break before she carried out the final instruction, then pulled back her arm as far as she could and flung it out to sea.

"Goodbye, Mo," she whispered.

As she turned to retrieve the cushion she saw Geoff making his way up to meet her with his customary air of competence. She watched him until he reached her.

"Are you OK?" he asked, taking the cushion from her. "That can't have been easy for you love?"

She pulled him towards her and kissed him.

"It's done," she said. "I'm fine. And thank you for doing this, for being so understanding."

He lifted a strand of hair from her face, pushed it behind her ear and returned her kiss with extreme tenderness. "That's what I'm here for," he replied. "By the way, that was some throw you performed there, I'm considering putting your name forward for the cricket team next season."

Lizzie burst out laughing.

"I think it's best I stick to making the sandwiches" she replied taking the flask from him and returning it to the backpack.

He took it from her and slung it onto his shoulder as they made their way arm in arm back across the beach to the car.

PIE DANCE

Catherine Wilson

It was his second wedding, and retirement party for the M.D.

This meant 300 to 400 invited guests, at the magnificent factory ballroom; an event to surpass any other held there.

Invited by a friend who worked there, who wouldn't want to go to such a 'do?'

Suitably kitted and shod, six of us arrived ready for the big night.

A bottle of Champagne each at the door was a promising start. The massive ballroom was beautifully decorated and a big band filled the stage; the tables suitably gracious.

In front of the stage, decorated food tables were stretched across the room.

The band played, and we all danced; and danced on; and on again, until it became obvious that there was something amiss, with bigwig heads together whispering, trying to look untroubled and super official.

It was announced that the caterers hadn't arrived. But, 'Not to worry folks, it's all in hand, saved by another company which is on its way.'

Half an hour later the food arrived, trundled across the hall in a train of covered bins. Everyone cheered. As the covers were removed they cheered louder amidst laughter and next, uproar.

The bins contained pork pies, thousands of them, petite and beautifully packed.

The purple faced officials did what they were supposed to do and officiated, loudly.

Waitresses were instructed to place small trays of pies on to each table. By now some of the guests were feeling peckish and munched the odd pie or two, washing them down with the champagne and wine.

As the band struck up again a few dancers helped themselves to a pie as they danced by the stage. Some were dropped, accidentally - or otherwise.

We sat down laughing, watching this weird and terrific pantomime as pies, like alien grey billiard balls, were waltzed and quickstepped across the floor; stilettos piercing or sliding over them.

The band stopped playing and guests were asked to sit whilst management explained that it had decided to move everyone into the twin bars next door, where free drinks and refreshments would be served until the floor was cleared. There was an undignified rush; expensive pockets and handbags stuffed with pies, to the unoccupied tables in the bars.

Meanwhile, with the honeymoon plane due to leave Baginton airport just down the road in two hour's time, there was a vociferous argument going on between the newlyweds, the bride threatening to go home with her parents. Meanwhile back in the ballroom, our own driver friend was having his own conflict. His wife didn't want to dance, her feet were hurting in her new shoes – but objected to him dancing with anyone else.

As he moved to defy her, she picked up the keys and tottered off to the car park. It was snowing, and our lift home, which was miles away, was at stake. We chased after her to persuade her to stay. To no avail; she sobbed angrily in the car until her husband came and took over. She had been drinking and couldn't drive.

The journey home was in memorable silence.

ORPHEUS IN THE UNDERGROUND

Mark Kockelbergh

On the escalator at Waterloo Station I hear the sweetest music I have ever heard. A simple melody, painfully beautiful. Or beautifully painful.

At the bottom, a busker plays the ukulele. He wears a pink hat made for the Financial Times. There's nothing in which to collect coins. Around his neck hangs a piece of cardboard on which is written, 'Have you seen Eurydice in the city of the dead?'

I walk to catch my train and the music becomes fainter. It reminds me of something, bitter yet sweet.

I lie in bed that night and reach out for the memory.

Yes, I remember. The time I said goodbye to Helen last year. In a restaurant beside the river.

"I must tell you, Helen. I love you."

"Please don't," she said kindly. "I'm marrying Simon next week."

It had been a hopeless romance. A chaste affair, we hadn't even kissed.

The next evening, I hear music again in the underground. It's different this time. Discordant, jagged with broken rhythms. At the bottom of the escalator is the busker again. His pink hat is made from today's FT, so he must make a new one each day.

Again the music triggers a memory I cannot place. In bed I remember.

I saw Helen again by chance, a couple of weeks after the night in the restaurant. She looked pale. I asked her how the wedding had gone.

"Simon ended it a few days before."

"I'm sorry." It was a lie.

"He didn't give a reason, the bastard."

She was clearly vulnerable. So, I took her to my flat, gave her a couple of drinks and slept with her. She remained silent throughout. After apotheosis, well mine anyway, I felt only disgust. I feigned sleep and heard Helen softly sobbing beside me. Next morning, she was gone.

One evening I talk to the busker.

"What's your name?"

"O," he says.

"O? What does that mean?"

"Nothing."

"Who's Eurydice?"

"Wife. Lost and gone."

"Where's the city of the dead?"

"Here."

"The underground?"

"Yes."

"I don't understand."

"My lyre," he says.

O looks apologetically at his ukulele.

"It charms the dead. If I play, they will come. I'll show you."

He walks to the platform and strums a chord.

"There. You see?"

He points to a young woman walking towards us.

It's Helen. Her face looks like a death's head. I stretch out my arms.

"Helen, Helen."

She looks straight ahead and says nothing. She walks past me, turns at the exit and is gone.

I look around. O stands at the edge of the platform.

"There. Eurydice," he calls.

He climbs down onto the tracks and disappears into the tunnel. I don't see him for several minutes. He walks back, alone.

I feel a blast of wind from the tunnel. I run to the edge.

"O, O, behind you."

He turns. A train roars out and rips him to pieces.

Later, there's a report in the paper. O's head and his ukulele were seen floating down the Thames. Under Tower Bridge, past Greenwich, into the estuary and finally out to sea.

BARNEY THE BASSETT HOUND AND CEDRIC THE PINK PIG

Jean Busby

John Bailey, a gentleman farmer was the local master of Poodleton Fox Hunt. He, his wife Sybil, and his two sons George and James also owned Overstone Farm in Poodleton.

Barney, their Bassett Hound dog used to lead the hunt with all the other dogs but now Barney was too old to race over the fields after foxes.

Barney had dark brown fur, large floppy ears and sad eyes and he was not very happy because he did not receive the same affection as the other Bassett Hounds. Most of his days were spent in the farm yard or near the pigsty and his only friend was Cedric. Cedric was a large pink pig with small fat hairy legs and a curly tail. His right eye resembled a black patch and grey bristles stood upright on his head. He was a happy smiling pig.

"Hello Barney why do you look so sad today?" said Cedric.

"Because no-one seems to want to bother with me anymore. I wish I could escape from here and find somewhere else to live," he said.

"I feel the same as you," said Cedric. "Only the other day I heard Mr. Bailey discussing with his manager about sending one of his pigs to the market. Robin Redbreast tells me that there is a Sanctuary Farm for animals a few miles from here. How about it Barney. Do you think that if we escaped from here that they would look after us? I need to plan the escape quickly as I think the pig they were discussing was me."

But before Cedric could plan his escape, the next day George and James drove their van with a trailer attached towards the pigsty.

"Come on Cedric," said George, as he opened the pigsty gate. "Get into the trailer."

Cedric tried to run away but the two men ran after him and managed with a board by the side of his head to guide him into the trailer. As they drove away all the other pigs began to cry. The trailer slowly disappeared on to the bumpy road towards the market but James was driving too fast and it detached itself and turned over on its side. Cedric made his escape and ran back to the farm to collect Barney, but Barney was not there.

"Barney where are you?" shouted Cedric. Barney ran from the open farm yard door towards him.

"Oh thank goodness," said Cedric. "We'll run across the fields to find the Sanctuary. Robin Redbreast will guide us."

Cedric and Barney ran over several fields and hid in a forest so that they couldn't be found. It was late evening when they arrived at the Sanctuary. Jane and Andrew Brewster a young couple, had only just opened Apple Tree Sanctuary a few months ago. Already there were horses, donkeys and several other animals that had been rescued by them. Cedric was so tired that he lay on his side and fell asleep. Barney was beginning to look exhausted.

"Good gracious what have we here, a Pig and a Bassett Hound dog."

Robin Redbreast explained what had happened and they quickly offered Cedric and Barney a new home.

George and James never did find Cedric so they hooked the trailer back onto the van and took another pig to the market. Mr. Bailey received rather a large sum of money for his pig. He was none the wiser that it wasn't Cedric and he never bothered to find out what had happened to Barney.

Cedric lived happily with all the other animals in the Sanctuary and Barney became Jane and Andrew's new loving pet dog.

BOOKWORM

Hazel McLoughlin

Today, she would read Therese Raquin again. Nora had always loved reading. She could still recall in those days before the intrusion of television, that warm contentment of an old armchair and a clutch of new library books. It was what had attracted her to James initially when they had first met in the College Reading Room. The memory seemed to tilt sideways now as she struggled to remember why she was lying on the floor on a lumpy carpet of old magazines and yellowing newspapers, with a kitchen chair sprawled untidily across her body. She reached out a hand to move it and was stilled immediately, like the game of "statues" she had played as a child. Spasms of pain ransacked her, giving no quarter. She lay still. She wondered how she might resolve the problem, hoping that a few moments of immobility would do it, but all the while knowing this was not something she could do on her own. Next time she'd choose a book from a lower shelf. A voice in her head reminded her that she should have known better.

In the house next door, Becky and Sam were having lunch. They had spent long, dusty hours when they had first moved in, knocking down the wall between the back room and the old scullery. Now the sun lightened and cheered their spacious kitchen. The home-made soup and freshly baked bread tasted all the better for it. The couple savoured the food and the chance to spend time together. Becky's duty roster at the hospital and Sam's university lectures did not always coincide favourably.

"I don't understand why that sociology book hasn't arrived yet," said Sam, "Especially when Amazon are claiming it was shipped at the end of last week. I could do with it for this next essay."

"Hope they haven't delivered it next door," said Becky. "In the six months we've been here, I've only ever seen that woman twice, scuttling to the shops and looking over her shoulder like some undercover agent. Remember, she wouldn't even open the door to us when we tried to introduce ourselves as her new neighbours. The only sign of life next door is the twitching of the curtain."

It was just over an hour later that Sam found himself opening the sagging gate and making his way up the dandelion spangled path to knock on the door of his neighbour. Behind the peeling brown paint, nothing stirred in response. He tried again, then turned to walk away, when some humanitarian, or even merely inquisitive instinct prompted him to lift the flap of the letter-box. Like their own house, the front door opened directly into the living-room, where his eyes were drawn to a sprawl of plump, black-trousered legs, protruding from an untidy spill of books. It reminded him of a cartoon. The emergency services were quick to respond and despite her confused reluctance, Nora was soon on her way to hospital. Sam waited while the broken window-pane was boarded up and signed to accept Nora's key in her absence.

The house smelt.

"Small wonder!" said Becky, with her nurse's nose for hygiene. "There must be years' worth of free newspapers and junk mail here, not to mention all these stacks of books. Do you think she's read them?" It was the day before Nora's discharge from the hospital. Becky had visited their neighbour several times, though the conversation had been one-sided and confined to practicalities. She and Sam had decided, with the casual rectitude of their age, that cleaning and tidying Nora's house might be a more appreciated neighbourly gesture.

They started in the kitchen, scouring mercilessly the black spores on the work surface and the tentacles of mould in the sink and sweeping the desiccated fly carcasses from the window ledge. The cupboards held only tins of soup and vegetables but still, despite their efforts, a smell of rot, like some medieval sewage system, persisted. Not daring to shift the hoarded newspapers and book towers, they moved, single file down the narrow corridors between them into the back room. Here, in the gloom, the smell hung, pungent and penetrating, potent as a plague visited on a Pharaoh. Sam moved to open the window. In his urgency, his foot caught the corner of a large book, causing the stack to topple, creating a domino momentum that shifted the landscape of books lying haphazardly on the floor. That was the moment he caught sight of another pair of legs, clothed this time in tatters of cloth, certainly not plump, for the shrivelled flesh barely covered the skeletal shanks.

The police came quickly. There was no need for an ambulance. And how Nora might have appreciated Becky and Sam's help remained a point of conjecture.

The scant explanation that emerged at her trial later centred around a life of scathing bullying and servitude, inflicted by an arrogant and controlling misogynist, posing as a husband. When he had fallen in an attempt to lift down a heavy book from a top shelf, Nora had gratefully accepted the opportunity to be rid of him. She had merely piled more books on top of him, like a funeral pyre and waited. Nobody missed him.

In her cell, Nora sits calmly on the bed. The prison library is well stocked and she has started an Open

University module on English Literature. She had, after all, long since resigned herself to a life without freedom.

And here, at least, she is free from that voice, the one that could only speak in the precisely modulated tones of mockery and contempt, in sound bites of sarcasm, the one that shouted and abused her from the grave of books, the one she ignored, the one that sank to a pleading whisper before it was silent.

A PTOLEMAIC TALE

June Bradley

She could smell the fires. Their pungent smoke permeated the air, usually fresh from the sea and sweet with Jasmine and Blue Lotus. This sweetness was malodorous. A scent of invasion. The scent of Rome.

For days now Samia had heard hushed voices and the soft tread of bare feet, then the gentle slap of oars as one by one boats left the harbour under cover of darkness. There were no longer guards to stop them. The hustle and bustle of a working palace had ceased. But she would stay; where else would she go? It had been her home for as long as she could remember.

She touched the first of sixteen columns that separated her quarters from the kitchen and bakery. Unlike the huge red granite columns that faced the harbour of Eastern Alexandria flanking the gateway to the island of Antirhodos and its palace, these surrounding the inner courtyard gardens formed a covered walkway around its perimeter and were adorned with brightly painted figures. She could feel the pigment beneath her fingertips, her memory instantly recalling their vivid hues and intricate patterns as she made her way barefoot along the colonnade towards her favourite spot outside the kitchen entrance. This was her special time of day. She had taken ownership of it, the hours before the sun rose to bake the Earth, before anyone else in the palace stirred.

She combed her fingers through the herbs as she passed their bed, mint, parsley and dill, coriander, fennel and bay, their scent momentarily fresh and invigorating.

Only the clicking of insect wings and rattle of fronds from the five monolithic date palms growing at the centre of the garden intruded into the silence as an inquisitive breeze disturbed the air. She stopped, pressed her body against the last column breathing evenly, nostrils flaring, ears stretching waiting for the creak of a leather sandal or the cadence of a drawn sword. But her instinct told her Octavian would want to relish his victory at Actium, his defeat of Egypt, the Queen and his brother-in-law. There was no need for stealth. His actions had shown his intention to humiliate her with as much theatre and pomp as possible. But he would be disappointed. Samia knew her Queen almost as well as she knew herself.

When the third daughter of Ptolemy XII was born, Samia at the age of fourteen was assigned to the Royal nursery as a servant. It became swiftly apparent she was a child with two faces. Over the years Samia had witnessed the best and the worst of her young mistress, who could be generous and loving but equally manipulative and ruthless. She was well educated, fluent in several languages and clearly the growing princess would be loyal only to herself and her ambitions. The Pharaoh's eldest daughter had already died and his second had been beheaded, at his consent, by the Romans. Consequently when he died the Princess at the age of eighteen was made co-Regent with both of her younger brothers in turn. Like father, like daughter so it seems as Samia had always thought their passing was both timely and convenient for the young Queen; though not entirely unsuspicious. It is said the fig never falls far from the tree and wisely she kept those thoughts safely locked away behind her slowly failing eyes.

Samia stepped back into the shadows and continued on her way from column to column until she reached the entrance to the Palace kitchen. She sat on the floor and leaned against the wall hugging her knees.

"May Nunnut protect us this night," she whispered.

Usually the residual heat from the fires and ovens that fed the Palace daily was held in the walls but tonight it felt cool through her linen shift. There was no mouth-watering smell from previously baked bread or roasted meat and the only sound was of inquisitive rodents inspecting the floor for grain and crumbs.

Often at dusk, one of the servants would be sent from the kitchen to her quarters with a basket of bread sweetened with honey or dried fruit and a beaker of beer to appease her growing taste for sweet foods and pleasant company. It was comforting to have the respect of age. She had served the Queen until this veil of Sindon had finally fallen across her eyes leaving her unable to care for the youngest child as he grew. She was grateful to have been given her own quarters, small but perfectly adequate, where she could hear the sounds from the great Portus Magnus Harbour of Alexandria. But there had been no visits from the kitchen yesterday evening or today. She had missed the company and had a desire for some sweetened bread.

She stood up, stepped into the kitchen and began to feel her way from bench to bench. The surfaces had not been cleaned. She rubbed the gritty flour between her thumb and fingers. It seemed that anything edible had been taken by the fleeing staff. Utensils and empty bowls littered the kitchen. At the far corner of the room she caught something with her foot. It rolled unevenly until it hit an obstacle. Samia squatted down carefully investigating the floor beneath the bench with her fingers until she felt the smooth leathery peel and calyx of a pomegranate resting against the leg of a stool. It had escaped the attention of the rodents who were probably after easier bounty for now. Placing it carefully on the bench she returned to the stool, which judging by its size and shape, had come from one of the Royal Chambers. She pulled it carefully from its hiding place.

Sitting on the seat was a basket draped with a piece of linen, a work in progress pierced with a needle and its length of fine flax thread. She lifted it onto the bench and removed the fabric. Honey and musk, the intoxicating perfume of ripe figs permeated her olfactory senses. She picked a plump fruit from the pile luxuriating in the velvety sensuous skin as she let it roll from one hand to the other. She cupped it in both and lifted it to her face inhaling its perfume greedily until she began to salivate. Clearly these had been overlooked in the haste to abandon the Palace. She covered them with the fabric and slowly slid her treasure along the bench until it was closer to the entrance, then placed it on the floor and resumed her position leaning against the wall. Piercing the skin, she split her prize in half and ate each piece slowly, allowing the flavour and texture of the sweet sticky pulp and seeds to linger in her mouth and on her tongue for as long as possible.

Samia heard the soft thud of surefooted paws as they landed beside her and smiled as she felt the fine texture of fur on her skin as the cat rubbed its head and shoulders along her forearm.

"Bastet! You've found me. And how is my little goddess tonight hmm?"

The cat wound herself around Samia's ankles before settling down at her side purring contentedly. It was a comforting sound on such a strange night.

"Are you my goddess of the home protecting us from evil or have you come as the lady of dread and slaughter to warn us of what tomorrow may bring?" She scratched the back of Bastet's head. "Either way my lady, hunting has been good for you in the kitchen tonight, you have a full stomach." Bastet turned onto her back, stretched then sat up and began to wash herself. "So beautiful yet so deadly, you are perfect for this place," Samia whispered. Both stopped and turned their heads at the sound, distant and barely perceptible. The cat darted into the herb garden as Samia closed her eyes in concentration listening to the patter of small sandaled feet making their way along the colonnade. As they neared she recognised the step and the young shaking voice.

"Bastet, where are you? Please come and play?"

"Philadelphos, is that you?" Silence. "It's Samia, where are you child and what are you doing out here?"

"Samia?" His voice was barely audible and threatening tears.

"Quickly. This way, by the kitchen." She could hear the quick slap of his papyrus sandals as he ran towards her. "Why are you out here alone my little prince?" She patted the ground beside her. He sat down and snuggled into her. As Samia wrapped her arms around him she felt his body shiver. "You're safe here little one, now tell me what has happened."

She kissed his bare head and tickled his nose with the end of his little beaded side lock. He smiled and looked up at her.

"I woke up and my stomach was rumbling. We didn't have any food yesterday; we didn't see anyone from the kitchen."

"Didn't your mother's servants bring you anything?" He shook his head. "And your brother and sister, where are they?"

"Their beds are empty. I could hear their voices but I couldn't find them. They were laughing and whispering together like they always do."

Samia held him a little tighter. "That's very cruel of them."

"I know I should," he continued, "but I don't like them very much. Selene whispered that the soldiers were coming and they would feed me to the dogs."

"What about Caesarion, where is your big brother?"

"I haven't seen him; perhaps he's with the priests at the temple."

She couldn't tell the boy that word had reached the Palace yesterday confirming Roman troops were marching on Alexandria.

"And your mother?"

He took a shuddering breath. She heard the fear and bewilderment in his voice.

"There were no sentries to open the doors to her chamber and I couldn't open them by myself. I could hear her voice and the other ladies so I banged on the door but they wouldn't open it. I sat on the floor and waited but they wouldn't let me in. Then Bastet found me, so we played for a little while. Then she left and I followed her to the courtyard."

She had only looked after this little boy for three of his six years, but a bond had formed between them and she had grown to love him like her own. Sometimes he would escape his nurse and visit her. Now it seemed the nurse had abandoned the children.

Although Philadelphos and the twins, Selene and Helios were sired by Mark Antony, Philadelphos was truly his father's son. He was broader and stockier than his brother and sister, who were finer boned and favoured the Queen. This little prince was lighter in colouring, his hair, when unbraided from his sidelock, held a curl and his nature was sunnier and more open. Samia could understand the attraction between the overtly masculine Mark Antony and her Queen; she would herself have chosen him over any of the shaven skinned, bewigged and kohl eyed members of the Ptolemaic gene pool, past or present. As for the Queen's eldest son Caesarion, Samia had never taken to him. She had tended him, fed and washed him, nursed him when necessary but he had always been a serious solemn child, slim of face and body, a child; who as he grew into puberty, observed far more than he ever discussed and refused to make eye contact when he did, a compliant consort for his mother. He was far more like his late father whose murder was the spark that ignited this raging fire and brought them all to their present situation.

Philadelphos sat up. "I'm very hungry." He whispered.

"Ah, we can do something about that," she replied indicating with a hand. "Just inside there is a basket of figs."

He smiled. "I like figs."

She lifted her arm, allowing him to stand and enter the kitchen. He returned holding six figs in his pleated white linen kilt and gave three to Samia as he sat down again. She passed two back to him.

"Eat them slowly; we will save the rest for the morning."

With their stomachs sated, for a while at least, they dozed fitfully. The boy; disturbed by night dreams, was restless and Samia locked on to every sound. She heard the cat before Philadelphos who, disturbed by the spitting and growling, sat up and pointed to the edge of the herb garden.

"I think Bastet has a serpent."

Samia stood up. "Hold my hand little one, we must find the stool in the kitchen and climb up onto a bench. It will be safer."

"But Bastet?"

"She will do whatever she needs to do for your safety. Hurry now!"

She made Philadelphos lie tight against the wall then

lay behind him. Better for her to be a victim of the serpent than the boy. Eventually only the steady breathing of her slumbering charge disturbed the silence and she began to relax, surrendering to a sleep of dark dreams and demons.

***

When they awoke the sun was rising. Philadelphos helped Samia down from their sanctuary and led her through the kitchen, watchful for the serpent's presence, but there was no sign of it. Full from the abundant supply of rodents to dine upon, it had probably found somewhere secluded to sleep and digest its meal, Samia assured him.

"We'll take the basket of figs to my room where it will be safer and have our own feast," she suggested.

But when they got to where she had left them, the basket, figs and piece of linen with its needle and thread had gone. In its place lay the body of Bastet, stiff limbed and milky eyed. Philadelphos cried out as he dropped to his knees and stroked the soft fur. Samia comforted the boy as he wept at the loss of his friend.

"She gave her life to keep you safe," she assured him. "The gods will reward her in the next life. Now, I think we should try to find the twins and then go to the Queen's chamber."

He nodded and took her hand as they made their way around the courtyard perimeter. The palm fronds rattled and clattered as a fretful breeze gathered strength, warning Samia to hurry. She stopped for a second and inhaled deeply. She could almost taste the metal and leather on the air and found her heart beating to the sound of distant marching feet. As they hurried through the deserted chambers and silent passageways she prayed for the gods to treat them kindly. Great change was upon them and Roman mercy was rare.

***

While this story is not a factual account of Cleopatra's death and the fall of the Ptolemaic empire, it is nonetheless based on historical facts of that time and is purely a work of fiction.

1. Antirhodos Island was in the eastern harbour of Alexandria, Egypt. It was part of Alexandria's ancient royal port called The Portus Magnus. A Ptolemaic palace was sited there and was believed to have been Cleopatra's royal quarters. According to historians it was probably abandoned soon after Cleopatra's death. It is believed the island sank in the 4th century A.D. when it succumbed to earthquakes and a tsunami following an earthquake in the Eastern Mediterranean in the year A.D. 365. The site now lies underwater near the seafront of modern Alexandria at a depth of approx 5 metres.

2. Egyptian palaces housed large gardens incorporating edible plants, fruit trees, vegetables and water gardens. Perfumed plants and flowers were very popular.

3. Cleopatra was born in 69 B.C. and was the third daughter of Ptolemy XII (Auletes) and his wife Cleopatra V (Tryphaena) thought to be his half-sister. There was also a younger sister and two younger brothers.

4. Octavian defeated Cleopatra and Mark Antony at the Battle of Actium in September 31 B.C. He was Mark Antony's brother- in-law; his sister Octavia was Mark Antony's second wife. After Mark Antony's and Cleopatra's death and his return to Rome he became

known as Caesar Augustus. This marked the end of the Roman Republic and the beginning of the Roman Empire.

5. Nunnut was the ancient Egyptian Goddess of the Night Sky.

6. Sindon (pronounced Sindone) is a fabric of fine linen used especially for shrouds. It was also used in a wad, roll or pledget of soft cloth usually doused in medicine, to fill wounds during surgery. It was also worn by the priests of Isis and considered to be a magical garment used by persons to be possessed by spirits and made to meet the gods.

7. Pomegranates were very expensive fruit grown for and only eaten by the rich.

8. Figs grow from spring to early winter but the spring harvest yields the sweeter tasting fruit. In ideal conditions fig trees live to 150-200 years.

9. Bastet was the ancient Egyptian Cat Goddess of the home, domesticity, women's secrets, fertility and childbirth. She protected the home from evil spirits and disease – especially diseases associated with women and children. She was a guide and helper to the dead in the afterlife. Also known as 'she of the ointment jar 'and also the lady of dread and slaughter'. There were severe penalties for injuring or killing a cat.

10. Philadelphos was Cleopatra's youngest child and with Cleopatra Selene and Alexander Helios (twins) were the children of Cleopatra and Mark Antony.

11. Caesarian was Cleopatra's oldest son and was the child of Cleopatra and Julius Caesar.

12. Sidelock – Egyptian children had their heads shaved with a small section of hair left to one side to braid with fabric or beads. Most adults shaved their heads (especially at court) for hygiene reasons and to help combat the heat. Wealthier people and those of the royal household often wore wigs.

13. Children wore sandals made of papyrus.

14. Legend has it that Cleopatra took her own life with venom from the bite of an Asp (an Egyptian Cobra) a large snake very similar to the Indian Cobra. Recent research and discoveries lead experts on the subject to a more likely conclusion. It is now thought that she could have administered poison by a) an ancient form of hypodermic needle; commonly used in the preparation of the dead, b) scratching herself with a sewing needle and dropping the poison into the wound, c) rubbing poisonous ointment onto her skin, d) taking the poison orally using opium, hemlock or wolfsbane.

Cleopatra died on August 12th 30 B.C. She was not Egyptian but was the last of the Macedonian Greek Dynasty to rule Egypt. Her children; sired by Mark Antony were taken to Rome and cared for by Mark Antony's widow Octavia. Caesarian; aged sixteen, was murdered by Octavian shortly after his mother's suicide. Alexander Helios died at the age of fifteen and Philadelphos at the age of seven. Their cause of death is not known. Cleopatra Selene married Juba the Berber King of Mauretania and had one son – Ptolemy of Mauretania, Cleopatra's only grandchild.

Egypt became part of the Roman Empire and the private property of the Emperor. It was the source of Rome's valuable grain supplies.

LOVERS REUNITED

Jean Busby

Oh friendly sea. As lovers we walk barefoot along the soft sandy shore on a hot summer's day, with not a cloud in the blue sky. A perfect day as the ripples of the white warm shallow waves creep gently over our feet. There's a slight breeze in the air. It smells fresh, so fresh that we can taste the salt on our lips. Patches of seaweed cover the small rocks. Seagulls fly above us squawking, almost as if they're inviting us to join them as they settle on the deep ocean.

Parents with younger children pulling them through the waves on plastic boats. The children screaming with excitement as the boats bob up and down. Surfers lie on their boards swimming towards the deeper rolling white waves of the ocean.

Strolling for a little while John turns and kisses me. He says, that he loves me even though we've been apart for 30 years, and that he's never stopped loving me. It's almost as if time has stood still and we're back again as teenagers without a care in the world. Gazing across the ocean the sunlight sparkles on the water, changing its colour from blue to green, then pink, with a touch of purple.

Still holding hands, we walk further out into the sea. The water becomes so deep that our feet cannot touch the bottom of the sea bed. We wait for a large wave so that we can jump over it.

One takes us by surprise driving us apart, rolling us underwater towards the bottom of the murky sand bed.

We laugh as we come up for air. As we swim and float on our backs the sun on the water streams down on us. It's as if we're sitting in a warm bath, so happy and content, wishing that it could go on forever, but nothing lasts forever.

Swimming towards the shore and lying on our backs water gently flows over us. We then decide to walk back to our hotel collecting shells as we do so. One is shaped like a snail lying in seaweed, another is shaped like a fan.

It's a beautiful warm evening as the sun goes down and the moon lights up the sky. We walk barefoot again along the shoreline holding hands. It's very romantic. He's everything that I could wish for a very loving man, a man that I want to spend the rest of my life with but I cannot. His hair has changed from brown to white over the years. Why did I leave him all those years ago?

He's taking something from his jacket pocket. It's a box containing a diamond ring. Tears come into my eyes as he places it on the third finger of my left hand. He says that he will return.

I say goodbye to him forever as he flies home to his wife and family. I know that I'll never see him again.

The next day with tears in my eyes I walk along the shoreline. I cannot bear life anymore without him. It's a windy day and it's beginning to rain. The sea has changed from blue green colour to almost grey. As the tide is turning the waves are rising like giant black and grey monsters from the bottom of the ocean.

"Come with us,' they say, "Come with us …"

Suddenly I walk calmly into the ocean sea bed. The water becomes deeper and deeper. I know that I am drowning but I feel no fear, only peace as the monsters guide me to another life.

ROGUE ELEMENT

Hazel McLoughlin

Thelma had arrived early and parked her blue Peugeot at an oblique angle in front of the entrance to the Centre. Her back wheel trespassed on the empty disabled space alongside. "Not my problem," she muttered to herself.

Her 'phone conversation with the Secretary of the Art Society had given her the room number, so she was able to make her way there directly. A couple of older men had arrived already. John, the Secretary to whom she had spoken on the 'phone, introduced himself and bade her welcome.

"And this is Alec," he said, "One of our longstanding members." Alec bowed his head shyly and muttered a greeting. ASD for sure thought Thelma and wasted no further social energy on the encounter.

She glanced round the room and settled on a table, out of the draught of the door, where the light was good, and with the proprietary boldness of a disembarking conquistador, bagged it for herself. From her bag she took a white coat, a relic from her days as a Secondary School Art teacher in an inner city war zone of a school. Experience in dealing with mucky, inept adolescents, creativity bypass graduates of the National Curriculum system, had taught her to err on the side of precaution. She set up her desk-top easel and occupied the rest of the table with an impressive range of acrylic paints and brushes.

Other members of the group started to arrive. And just as she had always raked an assessing eye over new intake

Year 7's, Thelma began to process the newcomers automatically and classify them in unflattering groups of her own devising. So, she was rather surprised when a meek looking, definitely flowers-in-a-vase lady pointed out, "Actually, Dorothy usually sits at that table."

Dorothy, kittens-and-a-ball-of-wool and beige permed hair nodded, with all the assertiveness of a runny egg.

"Well, she'll have to find somewhere else to sit then, won't she," said Thelma in her classroom voice. She'd forgotten to put her hearing aids in, so the volume was largely for her own benefit. She was happy to ignore the muttering that followed on the grounds of inaudibility.

At the end of the evening, she drove home, pleased as usual, with her achievement. When superiority was an issue, modesty was such an outdated virtue. It was important to impress her success on the other members of the Art Group. Just as well, she thought, since Jack, her husband was now conspicuous by his absence. In fairness, he'd been dead for two years, though she still hadn't forgiven him for giving up so easily after the diagnosis, and despite all the nagging she had invested in his cure.

This week was a Water Colour Demonstration at the Art Group, given by Arthur, a portly bulk of a man with hands like Christmas hams, who was respected for his delicate brush strokes and technical competence. His Lake District landscapes were always the first to sell at the Exhibition. Arthur placed the sheet of paper on the easel, striped it with water and with a deftness born of long practice began to apply the sky blue paint. He had just opened his mouth to explain his choice of method when a loud voice with a plangent twang of impatience interrupted.

"It's far better if you do wet on dry. You can always use a pipette like this if you need to water the paint."

Jaws dropped in unison.

The class looked on as Thelma strode to the front, pipette in hand, and then watched with Arthur as runnels of his blue sky dribbled down the page like rogue raindrops. After that, it was simply easier to help Arthur tidy away his stuff and let Thelma continue with the demonstration. After all, she had her opinions and others were entitled to them.

The annual Exhibition had always been an enjoyable event – a celebration of their work and a social opportunity for family and friends. Thelma arrived early in the afternoon to set up. Martin and Geoff, the practical brains of the Art Group were about to start hanging the pictures. Well trained over the years by domineering wives, they offered no resistance to Thelma's bullying, honed to razor sharpness on the strop of Year 9 bottom sets and allowed her to choose the most auspicious spots for her work.

The Raffle Ticket ladies, however, later in the evening put up a stronger resistance and remained deaf to her suggestions, despite their being offered in her authoritarian assembly voice, as to how they might improve their efficiency and profit levels. She left them to muddle through and went to stand, conspicuously, at the Secretary's elbow, as he introduced the Mayor who would officially open the Exhibition. Thelma smiled for the cameras. She was surprised to see red sale spots appear on paintings she had marked as C- and even more surprised when none appeared on her own A* work. "No accounting for taste," she thought, which led her also to offer critical advice to Joan on the consistency of her sherry trifle custard. Had not the Mayor's wife, still smarting from her social ousting at the opening ceremony, simultaneously complimented Joan on the very same trifle, a small fracas might have ensued, since the maker of the trifle could trace her family history back to the warrior Boadicea and would not be trifled with. She had the bosom to prove it.

Thelma never missed a Wednesday evening class. But she was slow to notice the declining attendance of others, whose more fragile self-esteem or capacity for social interaction had been reduced to rubble by her extreme interference and wrecking ball small talk. When the diaspora reached a critical point and only four members turned up one evening, John recognized the need for action. He had long been an avid le Carre fan. He could do George Smiley even though his Circus tradecraft was a bit out of date. Not trusting his IT skills – he couldn't remember how to delete a name from the e-mailing list, and secrecy here was paramount, he rang every member of the group with one notable exception and invited them to a clandestine meeting in his dining-room.

Victims all, too long flattened by Thelma's sledgehammer social skills, they spoke with one voice of anecdotal slight and oppression. They rose in revolt and voted for liberation.

When Thelma turned up, as usual on Wednesday evening, she read the typed notice on the door of the now dark and empty room. She scornfully decried the dilettantist artists and their wimpish lack of endurance that had contributed to 'the insufficient class numbers that rendered it financially unviable for the group to continue.' "Wouldn't last five minutes in a classroom, that lot," she muttered dismissively. She was unaware and might even have been surprised, that the same lot planned to regroup, reform and meet in camera on Mondays.

But Thelma consoled herself with the poster in the foyer, advertising the new Rambling Club for the over-60's. Never mind the arthritis and the rheumatism and replacement hips. It wouldn't take her long to sort them out and get them moving.

SPACE

Jean Busby

Am I the only one when sitting in a Planetarium that within five minutes when the lights are dimmed and the very relaxing voice proceeds to describe the galaxy, I fall asleep.

It must the comfortable seats and the beautiful sparkly stars in the sky that send me into a relaxing mode.

From my bucket list the wish is to install a Planetarium ceiling in my bedroom so that whenever I find it difficult to sleep, I can press a button and away I'll be. Trouble is that I'd probably never want to wake up!

IN A WIDE OPEN SPACE

Ian Collier

"Kali-mera? Was that closer today Maria?" asked Colin.

"Kaliméra Yes Mr Jones, you will be speaking like a native soon ha ha! Did you have a nice evening?"

"Oh yes, the olive grove was lovely at dusk, the colours in the sunset, the insects going quiet, the stillness, then as the moon was rising we saw a flock of bats. Is it a flock? Could be a murder, like crows?"

"I think it's a cauldron of bats Co..."

But before Caroline could finish Maria interrupted: "Oh Theo meeu—oh my God! They were flying away from you weren't they?" crossing herself three times as she spoke.

"Yes, well they circled a bit, then headed off towards the sea, didn't they love?" answered Colin. Caroline, helpfully chipped in, "We're on an island dear. Everywhere is towards the sea," and smiling.

"There's an old saying- when they come, the bats, they curse like rats: when the bats again go, the honey will flow. It's not exactly that, but you get the sense perhaps?"

Maria went back into hostess mode: "Now. Breakfast? You want cereals? One tea? One coffee? Bread? Honey? Toasted bread? Yes? I have some pastries too, I've made Daktyla today? We make drinks, and toasted bread, and bring them, other things on sideboard, help yourself."

"What is the plan today sweet?" asked Caroline as they feasted, "I'm already fifty shades of lobster- I can't spend another day on the beach."

"Exploration! We'll go boldly forth! If that's OK?

There was that car hire place we saw in the back street, get a little Fiat and scoot around, look at some of the villages?" Colin answered removing a sun hat to gently scratch his bald patch, a sun hat that should have been worn far longer than it obviously had been. "There's got to be loads of cute little villages up in the hills."

***

"There's got to be a catch, you know, it'll break down or something," Caroline cautioned.

"No, it's like the guy said, they don't spend money on a website, they just look at what Hertz are offering and undercut it. And we've got all these tokens too."

"Yeah, I bet they are all rubbish. I'll drive. You tell me what that map and the satnav says."

"Are women allowed to drive here?" Colin laughed, handing over the keys.

***

They turned into another little car park at the side of another small taverna. This one too was closed. Getting out, they laughed about the day so far, near-death experiences on hairpin bends, the satnav telling them they were passing a hairdresser which was in the centre of a wide-open space, not even a tree for miles, but the satnav insisted there was a hairdresser there. This village didn't exist for the satnav- nothing at all built up between the invisible hairdresser and a winery and museum five miles over the top of the ridge. So far the paper map was winning hands-down. The map said they were in Miliou Skoulíki. The sign over the door said they were at the Aima Taverna, Miliou. The notice on the door said they opened at 8 p.m. and the token in Colin's fist said they could have a free bottle of wine with an evening meal. They agreed to kill the 2 hours by walking around the village.

As they walked between whitewashed houses, along narrow twisting streets, they didn't see a soul. The village looked dead. A slight incline led up to a Greek church, the blue paint on its roof mostly gone, leaving only the flaking white undercoat. It was in a very poor state of repair, the windows cobwebbed over, not even boarded up.

Colin tested the gate and it creaked open easily despite the sound effects.

"Come away Colin. This place gives me the creeps and it's getting worse the closer we get. What you say, we go back to the digs, freshen up and go to the usual place, or how about we try the pizzeria?"

"Come on! We should explore. It's not like it's locked up or anything."

"Over my dead body!"

"Aw OK- we'll just wait till 8 for the free bottle of wine. You know me, always down to the last drop."

"Fine, but certainly not the church and I'm not convinced about that taverna either."

They walked back down the cobbled street, only pausing at the sound of a swish. Looking up they saw a couple of bats heading to the derelict church.

Eight o'clock came, and went. A few minutes later lights came on in the taverna and a neon sign over the door crackled and buzzed to life. Heavy bolts could be heard being withdrawn and the door opened inwards. A tall, thin man, with a grizzled beard poked his head out and glanced up to check the sign was working.

Colin and Caroline walked in. They were surprised that they weren't alone, but no one else had entered while they waited, yet half the tables and the bar were occupied.

The meal was delicious. A tad of garlic wouldn't have gone amiss, but otherwise very good, and the wine was one of the best whites they had ever had. Colin said that that in itself was almost worth the cost of the car hire, better than many of the bottles they had bought.

When Colin asked for the bill, the waiter said, "Tonight it is free, a tradition. There are a couple of deaths in the village." Caroline insisted he take a 20 Euro tip suggesting he could donate it to the families of the bereaved. The waiter smiled and thanked them.

Outside, their car was covered in bats, black squealing bats. Their snouts littered with sharp teeth, they stank fetid, like a rotting wound. A man walked from besides the car, he wasn't there- then he was- a tall thin man, his grizzled beard framing his snarling teeth.

The Joneses acting on pure instinct ran. They ran deep into the village, ever uphill. Most of the houses were still silent and dead; a few seemed to burst with laughter as they passed. Still they ran. They ran until they reached the town's pinnacle. Looking back down the cobbled street the moon illuminated the still snarling face as bats swarmed around him. Colin tried the gate again, and they ran up the steps, their pursuers had stopped at the gate.

Hope prompted Colin- "Do you think it might still be consecrated?" The tall thin man proved it wasn't by opening the gate.

Extract from the coroner's report.
The deceased were found at the bottom of a gorge. There were indications on the road above that a vehicle had breached the edge on the hairpin bend. The couple had been seen in a bar drinking wine the evening before their disappearance and based on that they are thought to have died 23 days before being found.

On impact, the couple, who had not been wearing

seatbelts, both passed through the windscreen, causing several major lacerations to the head, neck and upper chest. Despite only a smattering of blood at the scene, it is clear that they must have bled out quite quickly, although the infestation and scavenging by insects was negligible. The woman's fist was clutched around a 20 Euro note which has been passed on to the executors of the will along with their other personal effects.

THE GRAND NATIONAL

Mark Fletcher

When I think about where I grew up, I think about when I competed in the Grand National, and by that I mean, *The* Grand National, not that horse race they have on the telly. It was held on my last ever day in Hatchley-Green, four days shy of my fourteenth birthday. I didn't want to move, but Mum had been offered a better position at a hospital some hundred miles away. Before I was to leave, I suggested to the old gang that we do the Grand National, start to finish, the whole thing in its entirety, no ifs, no buts, and no short-cuts.

Now, the Hatchley-Green Grand National didn't involve horses, it was all about the individual, and it was staged in the urban sport that was 'garden hopping'.

Garden Hopping was an urban pursuit where those competing would have to run across as many front gardens as they could, without veering off onto the pavement. In some towns they call it 'hedge hopping', but I think that is too basic when referring to the Grand National, our one has it all, hedges, fences, walls, gates, ponds ... and a few disgruntled residents.

We had sat in the park the Friday evening before, going through the rules, there was only one really, anyone going onto the pavement before Mick's shop would be disqualified. Everyone present were in agreement. We sat there bragging about who would win, until it got dark, after that it was myself and Niall Reeves. My mum was pulling one last late shift, so I had no time to be back for, and Niall simply never wanted to go home.

The next day we assembled in the Rec, 10 am as agreed. There was a good turnout. I didn't think they'd all come, but lo and behold, they did, all seven of them.

There was David Mount, arguably 'the athlete' amongst us, a regular goal scorer for the local junior football team. He was clad in his red and white football kit scheduled to play that morning, he even still had his football boots on. Before he had trotted over, his dad had warned him to be quick, fearing he'd miss the kick-off. There was Scott and Jack Fenton. Jack was two years younger than us, in his first year at senior school, but he always hung around with us anyway.

Then there was Nick Craven. His parents weren't short of money, and my God didn't he know it, he was wearing his brand new Nike trainers, the ones he told us all week he was getting, complete with an Olive-green Ellese tracksuit, and a white Reebok baseball cap - you'd think he was a catalogue model.

Even Bobby Lawrence had showed. Don't get me wrong, he was always game for some mischief, but being the most overweight of the group made him a rank outsider in what was an event for only the most elite of urban athletes.

Jordan Miller was definitely a favourite, confident and bullish and - in his eyes, the leader of our gang, yet the first to whine when things didn't go his way.

Lastly there was Niall Reeves, still sporting the black eye that his dad had given him two nights before, I don't think he was particularly enthused about joining in the race, it was just a reason to get out of house.

***

As we're walking through the jitty into Halesford Avenue we have a recap, "Right" I announce, we'll start over the road in the next jitty, then we jump over into the first garden, and keep going all the way to the corner, 'round into Burling Road, then into Crowhurst Drive, before going straight u..."

Scott Fenton piped up "I thought we just goes to end of Crowhurst?" His face screwed up, before his brother Jack chimes in.

"Yeah, the gardens stop there, you have to go onto the path to get around 'Phone box man's' house."

"Not exactly..."

"Well we can't go through his back garden surely?" Bobby asked.

"Sure we can," I said, "His garden runs all the way along the side of his house, 'round to the front. Then we'll carry on up Whetstone Road, 'till we get to Mick's shop. *Then* we go on the path, up the jitty, across to the next jitty, and then into the Rec."

I pointed at the jitty we had just come through, "First into the Rec is the winner..."

All in all it was a basic route - excluding all the obstacles, but they were still strung up about going through 'Phone-box man's' garden. I try and convince them that he probably won't be in, being a Saturday.

"Course he'll be in," David Mount complained, "Policing that phone box is his life"

"We won't get that far anyway," Scott said glumly, "Someone always comes out by that point."

"My dad'll go mad if I'm late for the game too," said David,

"Well if you lot are too scared..." Nick said, baiting.

"Ha! Scared! I'll be the only one who finishes!" boasted Jordan, "No one else will have the balls..."

"Bet I finish before you," challenged Nick,

"A pound says you don't!"

"I'll bet you a tenner!"

Jordan said nothing, he just scowled. Nick boasting his wealth like he did, was always hard to argue with, not being his friend meant you didn't get to go around his house. And his house is great. It had everything, widescreen TV, hot-tub, but it meant nothing that day.

Jordan turned and points at Niall's trainers, the right sole of which was noticeably loose. "You're not getting far in them," he sneered,

"Looks like you've decided to wear your best clothes too," Nick says cruelly,

Niall just shrugged.

David got back to the matter at hand. "Right! Are we going to do this? Dad'll go mad if I'm late for kick-off. I told him that I left my football at yours," he pointed to the brothers, Scott and Jack, who lived on Lyman Close, just off Crowhurst, which was good, because if anyone should get recognised, it would be those two.

"Football!" scoffs Scott, as he switches his skateboard to his other arm. He was a worse player than me, but then I could never skate.

"I had to think of something"

"Cause if you get caught and miss football you'll get grounded," Nick jeered.

"What happens if you get caught? You lose your computer for a night?"

Everyone, apart from Nick laughed, before Jordan stepped forward,

"Right shut up everyone! We're faffing around and drawing attention. Let's get started."

Scott nipped up the jitty quickly to stash his skateboard in the hedge, same place he usually did if we were out Garden-hopping, or playing knock-and-run, which as it stood, he is the champion of, based on the length of the driveway; but that's another sport all together. Nothing was said until he re-joined us. We each stood with one hand on the small fence. The driveway of the garden ahead is empty - a good start, but they have a willow tree before the next garden, so after that it was a mystery tour.

Over the road on the driveway next to the other jitty, the old man who lived there had come out to see what we were doing, no age to pursue us but hoping to be a deterrent anyway. Just up the jitty we'd come through, stood Sophie Harrison and Carly McGoldrick, who have agreed to witness who wins by staying there till we come back around, they were both pretty-ish, and not exactly in the popular crowd, and none of us had made a move. It was rumoured that Sophie liked Nick, and Carly liked Jordan, at least that's what they both thought.

Thankfully it didn't dissuade the others, although it called for a hasty start, I turned back to the group to start the proceedings...

***

And we're off, I'd like to say that the start was filled with suspense, but with our unwanted spectator, the start became somewhat rushed. No sooner had I turned to the guys and said 'Right...' Jordan had taken it upon himself to bellow out a quick "Ready, Set, Go!" Even then, he swung his leg over the fence before finishing what he was saying. He claimed to be the best at everything, yet he always needs some sort of upper hand. He'd be calling for a restart if one of us had done that.

All the same, we're off, and our knees bang simultaneously as we all clamber over the waist-high fence that starts off the race. There wasn't nearly enough room for us to all to get over at the same time, and it's me who falls at the first hurdle. With Bobby one side, and Jordan the other, I found myself squashed between them both as we went to go over the fence, leaving me with a leg stuck on either side. As they both pulled away, I kind of fell down onto the driveway, unhurt, but clearly in last place as the rest racers ran off, giggling, on their way into the next garden, the hanging willow parting in various places as they did.

I had no time to lose, I got back up to my feet, my heart racing with adrenaline, I cast a quick glance at the old man over the road, his hands still on his hips, shaking his head as our eyes met. I should feel bad, I remember how he always used to say 'Hello' whenever I walked past to go to the Rec, but any feelings of remorse had to wait. I darted off across the front garden, through the hanging willow and into the next one. I landed on my feet this time, with just a few leaves in my hair. The rest were two gardens ahead. I raced across the lawn, over their drive - also absent of its car, I wondered how many of them would end up veering onto the pavement to get around the driveways that would have vehicles on.

I had serious ground to make up, so I didn't hesitate as I leapt the small wall into the next garden, simply by putting both hands on top, bounding over the same way Chris Eubank used to do when he entered the boxing ring. I could see now that I was only a garden behind both Bobby Lawrence and Jack Fenton, with one being the more obese, and the other being two years younger, it was vital that I beat these two. I raced through the next garden, jumping the knee-high wall that separated it from its neighbouring one, I had to swerve to prevent myself from careering into the round rosebush bed that sat in the middle of the garden. Just as I thought I'd avoided it I felt my tracksuit bottoms catch on the thorns, pulling away, I heard a tear, but didn't care for the damage, I couldn't afford to stop and assess it, for more reasons than just making up ground.

"Stop right there!!!!"

A voice screeched to the left of me, I looked to see the inhabitant of the house emerging from the side, a tall, thin lady talking in a posh accent, as if she wasn't from around here, kitted out in her marigolds and armed with her shears. It was a shame she hadn't pruned her bushes before the race got under way. Her shouting stops me in my tracks momentarily. She charges, trying to grab my arm with one hand whilst waving her shears in the other, I jump over the wall into the next garden, her shears missing my head by an inch. I quickly look over my shoulder; she'd only gone running to the end of her drive, around the wall-post and into the one I'm in. I wasted no time and darted across the lawn, over the picket fence and into the next, dodging Bobby and Jack, who had stopped to look back and see what the commotion was,

"Laters!" I shout, as I raced across the gravel -laid frontage before jumping the wall into the next garden – the last one before it rounded onto Burling Road, Bobby and Jack burst out laughing as the lady with the shears came running across the garden before. I heard their feet turn in the gravel as they set off again. As I raced across the lawn Road, Scott Fenton and David Mount were both poised on the small fence ahead of me, a leg either side looking back at the house's front windows, at one of the windows as a large bald headed man was leaning out;

"Stay there!" he roared, pointing as he did, before his head turns to see me running across his lawn, "And you!" he bellowed. I did the opposite and threw myself over the fence, following Scott and David who were just ahead of me giggling. We looked back and saw his front door open as Bobby and Jack came running past.

"You've gotta be bloody kidding?!" He exclaimed out loud, at the sheer audacity of Bobby and Jack choosing to carry on, rather than bow out of the race. Me and Dave had both turned, both in fits of giggles; Scott had paused briefly just to make sure his brother wasn't in any danger of being caught, he knew that if Jack were to get caught, then no doubt he would be getting thrown under the bus.

***

We were off again. Me and David were neck and neck. I heard Scott shout to Jack to hurry up before turning to run. The duty of care to his brother, combined with his commitment to the race was nothing short of admirable, but I was hoping that it would work to his detriment. Me and David hurdled the next wall simultaneously, The front garden was completely block-paved, to accommodate the two cars that are both there. We weaved in and out of them before jumping into the next one, which was also block-paved, although they had no cars that I could see, possibly had it done just to keep up appearances. I hadn't expected David to be trying so hard, in order to save himself for the day's game but he was giving it his all. I was glad that he had stayed in his football boots; he might be fast over grass, but on block-paved - or gravel frontages, he's well out of his comfort zone. I inch past him just to see a lady stood in the window with her hands on her hips, looking in disgust as me and David run past, Bobby and the Fenton brothers in tow, no doubt already perched there after the other three had run past - who I can see are only a few gardens ahead, up to their knees in the 'long grass'.

Just as we jumped the wall into the next garden I heard a roar...

"GET HERE!!!"

I turned to see the big bald man from the corner of Halesford charging up the driveway behind, even redder than before, angry that none of us had stopped when told to, and even angrier that he had had to pursue us. Me and David watched as Bobby, Scott and Jack clambered over to where we were, the man's hands gripped the top of the small fence, before he realised that he was not going to be successful without causing any damage. We jumped over the next few gardens, none of us daring to look back, but we could hear him panting out loud as his feet smacked the pavement, trying to keep up. When we had laid out the rules of the Grand National we all agreed to no setting foot on pavement, and with this guy after us, the rule wouldn't be getting broken anytime soon.

Me and David jumped into the next garden, the one with the long grass. We had never actually seen who lived there, the house looked so out of place on Burling Road, with its overgrown lawn and its 'tattier than tatty' privet hedge. The house itself was in dire need of a paint-job, the net curtains were filthy, and the windows were only single glazed. It used to be a dare to knock the door on Halloween, but after hearing a loud barking from behind it one year, we had since stayed away.

We both waded through the long grass, which was a precarious task, what with all the morning dew still present; the protection from the sun the hedge had given it prevented it from drying, and then there were various brambles and thistles that are also in the undergrowth. I grimaced in pain as I felt thorns pricking me, not just on my legs, but on my arms too. I'm wishing now I'd worn long sleeves, what with being a short-arse.

I felt my tracksuit bottoms becoming sodden, wondering if maybe David was better for being in shorts, but as he tripped I heard him cry out as his hands had gone into some nettles. I stopped to contemplate whether I should have helped him up, before Bobby, Scott and Jack came piling over the wall, all three falling around me and David. As much of a calamity as this was, we were all back onto our feet pretty quickly, sure that we could hear the bald man on the other side of the privet edge, now level with us. As we ran towards the next wall he rounded the hedge, blocking off us off from the path.

Fortunately for us he didn't know the rules, and with none of us ready to be disqualified yet, we jumped over the next wall, all apart from David, who had lost one of his football boots in the long grass; they were giving him a disadvantage over hard surfaces, but he wouldn't be faring any better with just a wet sock as a replacement. Me, Bobby, and the Fentons all froze as the bald man charged past the previous driveway, towards the garden we were in. Just as we thought he was going to come at us he saw David behind him, cornered, still in the long grass.

"Got you now you little bastard," he panted, happy that he now had a scalp, no longer having to run. We didn't move, we just sympathised at David's slimmer than slim chances, hoping he could at least get out and onto the pavement, there would be no shame in him bowing out that way. I glanced back ahead to see that Jordan, Nick, and Niall had all stopped in the last garden on Burling Road, where the garden runs along the side of the house, before it continues around the front onto Crowhurst Drive. All three are looking back too, wondering if this was the end for David.

The house's weathered front door opened, squeaking loudly as if it hadn't been opened in years, we saw a middle-aged man emerge, with a shock of shaggy grey hair, and glasses with thick lens; from a few metres away it looked as if they were taped at the side to keep them intact. He looked totally bewildered as to what he was seeing;

"What's going on here?" he screeched angrily. Before the bald man could answer, a great big dog – which I now know is an Irish Wolfhound, came bounding out, its bark echoing over the street. With David frozen in the long grass, the dog leapt up at the bald man – who couldn't get his words out, who put up his arms in defence. The dog got up on its hind legs, making as big as his dance partner, and that was literally what it looked like, as if they were doing a waltz, as the bald man tried to keep the dog's paws off him. David chose the moment to emerge out of long grass past the man in the doorway, who hadn't noticed him until then.

"What the...?" he exclaimed, but David was gone, having no choice but to leap the small wall, what with the dance going on in the garden's official entrance. As he rejoined us, I noticed that he hadn't salvaged his lost boot. We all turn and ran, going through the next couple of gardens with little trouble, I looked ahead to see that the front three have rounded the corner onto Crowhurst Drive, but there was still plenty of time to make up the lost ground.

***

As the front three rounded the corner, I thought I had heard a girl shouting, but I wasn't sure, what with the fiasco going on a few gardens back. Before we entered the side garden of the house we were yet again made to stop in our tracks as a car screeched beside us. This time it wasn't a resident who had unwittingly bought a property that was host to this prestigious race, but David's dad Alan, AKA 'Angry Alan', track-suited and red-faced, about to have one of his infamous 'nuclear meltdowns'. He got out the car, steam pretty much coming from his ears;

"What the bloody hell are you doing? It's nearly kick-off!" he yelled, too irate to even register the pandemonium going on back down the road. He scowled at the rest of us before looking back at David, who trotted towards the car, head down, and officially out the race. As Alan went to get in the car he is beckoned back from where we have come;

"Excuse me, your son - yes him, ran right through my rosebushes!"

It was only the lady with the shears. None of us had expected her to give chase like she had, and with that we all turn and race off towards the corner, as we do, we hear Alan shout back, "Sod your bloody rosebushes, I'm two players down as it is!"

Alan's car door slams, and as his car accelerates past us, we hear through the open window, something like, 'Where's your other bloody boot?!'

We couldn't help but laugh as we ran, Angry Alan was usually just all bluster if anything, David would most likely have to borrow a spare pair of boots, and should the team win, no doubt all would be forgiven. As we approached the corner I felt a pull on my shoulder. Bobby, who I'm surprised is still in the race, pulled me back in order to get ahead, a tactic regularly employed in order to compensate for his lack of pace. It did little good though because just as he tried to round the corner into Crowhurst Road, he skidded onto his side, the left side of his body embedded in a round flower bed – thankfully not one with rosebushes. I jumped over him and rounded the corner with Scott and Jack, only to come face to face with Kerry Prescott standing on the garden path, and Nikki Mabbutt, standing in the house doorway – still in her bedclothes, Kerry and Nikki were arguably the two prettiest and most popular girls in our year group, the kind of girls that you always tried to look cool in front of, yet here we all were garden-hopping, on Nikki's garden no less.

"Get off my parents garden!" screamed Nikki,

"You lot are so bloody immature!" shouted Kerry

"Nice Slippers!" Scott retorts, as we run past, making us laugh harder than what we already were after Bobby's exit from the race. The three of us barely made it over the wall before we heard another shout, this time from over the road,

"Oi, what you think you're playing at?!" Duncan Grimshaw was over the road, sitting on a scrambler motorbike that he didn't even have a licence to ride, presumably visiting his grandad. He was a lot older than us, having left school last year, although I think he dropped out a year early – possibly due to him breaking the windows in the Science block during the summer holidays. Yet a couple of pretty young girls angered at our tomfoolery had given him some self-righteous notion that he could somehow be a knight in shining armour. Still, I didn't want to stick around and receive a clout off him, plus we were closing in on the others. The three of us all decided to ignore him and carry on across the next garden.

Two gardens ahead were the other three, running across two joined up front gardens that are both mown to the standard of a bowling green. As I they raced across the grass I saw Jordan trip Niall up, sending him flat on his face. This only made me more determined to win, or at least beat Jordan. I could understand Bobby trying to gain an advantage, but Jordan claimed to be the best at everything, so to see him cheat in such a way was infuriating. As me and the Fentons reached the lawn, Niall was still on his knees spitting grass cuttings that he had almost swallowed on impact; the guffaws of Jordan and Nick can be heard as they jumped into the next garden.

The roar of Duncan Grimshaw's motorbike made me

turn around and see him coming up the first driveway and across the connecting lawns. Me and Scott both grab an arm each of Niall, pulling him up to his feet as Duncan came racing towards us, skidding across the lawn and falling off his bike, causing more damage in one move than the eight of us had so far in this race. We all jumped yet another small fence into the next garden, bracing ourselves for the one that followed - *the home of a thousand gnomes.* That wasn't our name for it, it was the sign that the man had on his front wall. The front garden hadn't got that many, but I'd say that there are well over a hundred or so, and there would've been more had he got the space, God only knew what his back garden was like. Before jumping the wall I saw Jordan step on the small, wooden imitation wishing well, that was in the garden, to give himself a better leap over the hedge, breaking its small apex roof. Up until then we hadn't caused any damage, and Jordan really didn't need to give himself such an advantage, what with having longer legs than any of us. I manoeuvred around the gnomes as if they were landmines, as does Niall and Jack, but Scott trips over one, grimacing as his hands - although protecting the rest of his body, embed into the assorted aggregates that filled in any space that weren't taken up by a garden ornament. I go to look back, but the banging at the house's window tells me to keep going, fearing that whoever got caught would be getting billed for damaged well. I notice that Jack - despite his brother looking out for him earlier, had decided to keep up with me and Niall and jump into the next garden, although it doesn't quite work out for him.

"Get here!"

Duncan Grimshaw, who after coming off his bike, had opted to pursue on foot, unbeknownst to us, had kept up alongside us on the pavement, seizing the opportunity to grab one of us; typical for him, he goes for the smallest in

Jack, who squeals as Duncan pulls his t-shirt. Jack pulls away briefly only for Duncan to again grab him by the wrist. Just as I was thinking as to whether I should help, Duncan puts his hands to his face. Scott, back on his feet now, has thrown a handful of stones at Duncan, the same aggregates that he'd just fallen in, before jumping over the wall to help his younger brother. Duncan is clearly bigger than either of them, but Scott uses the wall to jump into him like a professional wrestler as they tussled on the floor. Jack decides not to abandon his brother this time, wasting no time in helping his brother as the three of them scrapped like wild dogs. Me and Niall looked at them, before looking at each other. As if in silent agreement that the Fenton brothers would be able to hold their own, we proceeded over the next two gardens, two more to go before Whetstone road. Me and Niall are both panting, but with Jordan and Nick only a garden ahead, we dug deep. There was a sports car in the garden that Jordan and Nick were in – the last one on Crowhurst drive, just as I was wondering as to why they'd stopped, Nick bangs his palm on the car bonnet setting off the alarm;

"STOP! MOVE AWAY FROM THE VEHICLE!!" An American voice sounds out. It wasn't the first time we'd heard it, David's football had hit it once, setting it off. It have been amusing back then, but doing it the midst of the Grand National was certainly not the right time. It seemed like the pair had plotted this on approach, hoping that by doing so would make me and Niall disperse, as after this garden stood the high fence that led through 'Phone box man's' garden. As the car alarm gets louder on our approach, me and Niall run either side of the car, him closer to the house and me closer to the pavement. I stuck my head out past the high fence and glanced down the road, I could see a couple of young kids on the corner where the phone box was, giving me hope before we both took a run-up in order to ascend the high fence that Jordan and Nick had just disappeared over.

***

Just as me and Niall climbed up the fence we heard a roar from the side of the last house whose garden we had just left. It was 'Crazy legs' Tony! We all knew of him; there was rarely a day where you didn't see him out running, sweatband and all. We'd always opted never to antagonise him after David's older brother Craig had once told us how he'd been chased by him for well over an hour after pelting him with a snowball mid-run. Each time they thought they'd lost him, he'd re-appear, hot on the trail, all the way back to his house. If he'd knocked the door instead of running straight through the Mount family home in pursuit, then maybe justice would've been served. Instead, Tony got told where to go - and some, in the form of one of Angry Alan's nuclear meltdowns.

Tony came racing down the side of his house. He wasn't in his usual get up, but track-suited and in trainers, nonetheless. He tried to grab our legs, but we never gave him the chance. As we dropped down into 'Phone box man's' garden we found that Nick had landed in a bucket of Creosote, and it'd splashed all up his tracksuit! He stood there in pure shock, looking himself up and down, his trainers also ruined. With Tony's car alarm sounding off we never got to hear it when it happened, but we had a full view of the aftermath.

"Nice tracksuit!" laughed Niall as he raced off. Any attempts at keeping a straight face by me were thwarted from his remark as I followed him around the side of the house to the front garden.

As we got to the front of the house we could see Jordan three gardens ahead, firmly in the lead, and on the final straight that was Whetstone Road. Never before had we made it this far, but it wasn't over yet, 'Phone box man' was storming back to his front garden, after seeing off the youths on the corner, who were no doubt using the phone box to make prank calls. No sooner had you pressed the first digit and he would out like a shot. He saw me and Niall jumping the wall into his neighbour's garden, looking back at the phone box, then back at us, bewildered as to what he was witnessing. Before he could say anything, he was knocked off his feet by Crazy Legs Tony, who had rounded the corner too fast. Both lay there in a heap as me and Niall carried on across the gardens. There were only about ten to go but Jordan was still way ahead, we saw him disappear through a row of conifers that lead to the penultimate garden, I looked back and see Tony helping 'Phone box man' to his feet, before starting to run again.

"Shit, he's still coming!" cried Niall, but thankfully the next few gardens had no fences or walls; had there been then we'd have been caught for sure. We approached the conifers and I'm thinking how Jordan must surely be at the Rec by now, basking in his glory, although I couldn't yet feel disheartened as it had become more than just a competition between friends, what with Tony now coming across the front gardens in hot pursuit. Me and Niall braced ourselves as we both jumped through the conifers, hoping our chosen gaps would be as branch-free as possible. As we came through the other side we found ourselves faced with a car and a bucket of soapy water that had been spilled all over the driveway. The owner of the car, a middle-aged man, was standing over Jordan, who seemed to have banged his shin on the car's tow-bar, screaming like a banshee as he rolled around on the floor. The man was in the process of calling Jordan a 'silly bastard' until me and Niall came through.

"What the...??"

We didn't hang around as we both ran around the front of the car. The man was in store for another surprise though as Tony came charging through after us;

"What the hell's going on?" he shouts, only to be ignored as Tony followed us into the final garden before Mick's shop. We had to go through yet another row of conifers, but we knew that this time it led onto a massive lawn, the driveway being on the other side. What we didn't anticipate though was Daz the window cleaner doing his round. We both go to swerve around his ladder as it is propped against the house, but Niall's foot clips it, making the ladder wobble. Daz who's halfway up it calls down.

"Oi! I know who your dad is!"

We're both on the final stretch, both exhausted, but Niall couldn't help but turn around and shout back;

"Yeah, he's an arsehole ain't he?"

We both turn and race around the fish-pond that is in the centre of what was a huge front garden;

SPLASH!!

We look back to see that Tony, has come crashing through the conifers and straight into Daz's ladder, causing the window cleaner to fall off, and into the pond. Tony, having banged his knee on the ladder had also gone stumbling into the pond, as he had tried in vain to stay on his feet. Me and Niall race onwards across the only bit of pavement before the jitty, I'm just ahead of him and can picture myself now, running into the Rec as the victor...

***

"Martin!!!"

I stopped dead before the jitty as my mum was coming out of Mick's shop.

"What the hell are you doing? I've just come looking for you. I thought you were just saying goodbye to your friends??"

"I am," I stammered. I turned to Niall, who automatically puts his hand out. I shake it firmly.

"All the best" he says breathlessly.

"And you" I say.

We both hear activity from the big house's garden. No doubt Tony and Daz are both out of the pond.

"Good race," smiles Niall as he turns and races up the jitty, Mum doesn't ask what we've been up to, she just tells me to get in the car.

Mum set off down the road, back home so we could finish getting everything together before we left for good. She looked tired, what with her working late the day before, and making sure everything was ready for today, and although I felt bad that she has had to come out and fetch me like this, I felt a lot more disappointed in that I had only came in second place in the Grand National.

As Mum drove back from where I had just come, I got to reflect over the course in its entirety, I saw Crazy Legs Tony and Daz the window cleaner arguing on the big front garden, both dripping wet, the owner of the house trying in vain to be a mediator, and in the garden before that I see Jordan still crying, and with Mum's window down I hear him pleading with the man who had been washing his car, trying to make out that he was being chased. No doubt he'll shop us all in should his mum get called.

Before we turn onto Crowhurst Road I see 'Phone box man', holding Nick by the arm, he looks a miserable sight, his tracksuit now more tie-dye than plain.

As we round the corner into Crowhurst Drive, Tony's car alarm is still going off, whilst two gardens along, it looked as if Duncan Grimshaw, a neighbourhood bully, had come up short as Scott and Jack were both on top of him fighting furiously, the neighbours pleading for them to stop.

"Good Lord, is that Scott and his brother?" Mum asks

"The other guy started it," I mumbled, trying to hide my smile. Two gardens down I saw the gnome man out in his garden, assessing the damage to his wooden well. I felt bad for him, and even worse when I saw the giant skid mark that scarred the two connecting lawns, Duncan's bike still lying on its side.

As we approached the corner of Barling Road, I saw Bobby Lawrence, sitting on the edge of the kerb, oblivious to Kerry Prescott and Nicky Mabbutt, shouting at him from the garden of the flower bed that he had come a cropper in. He caught sight of me as we passed, giving me a thumbs-up as he rests there, content with the valiant effort that had given.

Lastly we saw David Mount, on the pavement outside the house with the long grass. Clearly no-one had a spare pair of boots. The owner is stood on the driveway, one hand on the collar of his dog-come-beast, the other hand pointing angrily at David. Opposite stands Angry Alan, pointing back angrily;

"I understand that, but he needs his football boot, it wouldn't be an issue if you actually cut your lawn!"

It was funny watching Alan taking the high ground, but make no mistake, David will be in hot water for this. He spotted me and Mum going past, and couldn't help but smirk as Alan ranted away behind him.

***

We bypassed Halesworth Drive as it's dead-end, which was just as well; if there was ever a reason not to return then it would be because of that lady with the shears. We proceed on down Burling Road, all the way to the bottom. As we got closer to what is now set to be our 'old' home, I saw three figures emerge from the main entrance of the Rec, Sophie Harrison and Carly McGoldrick, both walking either side of Niall. Clearly they had waited as requested, and they got to witness first-hand Niall as he came through the jitty for a grandstand finish.

I smiled to myself as we go past, he'd always fancied Carly, and both of them seem equally intrigued in what he is saying. No doubt it was his tale of triumph, and to be fair, he'd earned it. I think about school, when Mr Latimer had told him – unfairly in my opinion, that he would never amount to anything. Yet there he went, Niall Reeves, winner of the Hatchley-Green Grand National, and as we got closer I noticed him holding Carly's hand, I thought about how I had helped him up halfway through the race, sacrificing my own position, and would I do it again? Yes I would. I leant out the window, despite Mum telling me not to, my thumb in the air.

"ALL THE BEST CHAMP!"

THE HOUSE

Jean Busby

Very often I dream of the large modern Georgian styled house where I once lived with my husband and three children happily for 24 years. But there's another door that I open – it leads to a large ballroom in a mansion. Chandeliers hang from the ornate plastered ceiling. All around the room are people seated on red velvet settees and several of them are dancing to the quartet of musicians playing nearby. The ladies look so graceful in their panniered silk brocade sack backed trained dresses. The men wear long silk coats and elaborate embroidered waistcoats. Both men and women wear wigs.

He bows to me and takes my hand as we dance to the music. He is so handsome as he smiles. He says his name is Jonathan. I've met him before.

"May I have the next dance?" he asks.

Then after we've danced a slow dance very closely gazing into each other's eyes oblivious to anyone else, he takes my hand and guides me through the large open windows of the ballroom into a beautiful terraced garden. It's a warm summer's evening and the moonlight is shining on us. Nearby is a rose bush. He picks one for me and as I hold it in my hand and smell the open white perfumed rose, he takes it from me and places it in my hair. He leads me down to a large lake – white swans swim gracefully in it raising their long narrow necks swimming towards us. He kisses my hand and tells me he loves me and wants to marry me. I'm so happy but before I can answer, "Yes," it all disappears and I'm once again in my modern house.

I recognise the kitchen with its long island placed in the centre. I'm preparing a meal but a stranger says, "It's not your house anymore, it's ours."

I don't recognise him so I run upstairs to my old bedroom still furnished with the same Georgian chest of drawers, large wardrobe, and brocade curtains, but the ceiling is not there. I run down the large staircase into my arched hall, and I say, "No! This is my house."

As I walk through the Georgian door I glance up at the bedroom window and I see Jonathan. He's beckoning me to come back, but I can't go back. He disappears from view. I walk onto a large bowling green lawn and to the right are a row of thatched cottages.

"Some people say that we have had past lives. Perhaps I did live in Georgian times."

Was the Mansion here and did I live there with Jonathan or with my parents and siblings?

I always seem to dream about this house whenever I've been through a stressful time. Did my dream really happen? Was I happier then compared to the present times?

McGONAGALL'S GHOST

Mark Kockelbergh

"When Jack awoke, he remembered nothing. Except the dead dog."

Saul moved his lips as he read the words silently again, trying to get a feel for the rhythm of the line.

His wife glanced up and rolled her eyes.

"Are you writing that book of yours again?"

"Just trying out a line."

"And how many lines have you written so far?" said Kate.

"Roughly? One."

"One line? Really?" she said, her eyebrows raised in mockery. "That's impressive. You've obviously been able to give it your full commitment now that you're out of work."

"Not out of work," said Saul, "I'm just taking a few months off while I write my novel."

"And of course, we have only one income in those few months. Mine. Good thing I'm doing all this overtime, isn't it?"

"I know that. But I'm carpeing the diem. You know, seizing the day."

"I know what it means," she said coolly. "I'm going to bed. Early start at work tomorrow. You coming?"

"No, I'm going to stay up for a bit."

He sat down at the kitchen table and turned on his battered old laptop.

Saul had always wanted to write but life had got in the

way. University, job hunting, marriage, children. Now he'd done it at last. Quit his job in order to begin his novel. Like Gaugin in a way, chucking it all in to paint glowing, bare-breasted women in the South Seas.

But where Gaugin's paintings hang in galleries around the world, Saul had written one line. And he wasn't sure about that. It was about a dead dog after all. It wasn't as easy as he'd thought.

But at least he had his ghosts, his literary ghosts. Dead writers who'd met dismal ends.

There was Hemmingway, shot by his own hand. F Scott Fitzgerald, dead from alcohol at forty. Edgar Allen Poe, raving in a gutter in Baltimore. Christopher Marlowe, stabbed to death over the reckoning of a meal. Gogol, starving himself to death in his forties.

"Well, gentlemen," said Saul aloud, "what do you think of my first line?"

One by one they appeared. There were three of them tonight. Hemingway, Fitzgerald and Poe.

"I like it," said Hemingway, dressed in a khaki safari suit and sporting a white beard.

"I don't," said Poe. He wore an inky cloak to match his black eyes and luxurious moustache.

"Well, what do you know? I still don't know what The Raven was about. You agree with me, don't you Scott?"

Fitzgerald, a glassy look in his eye and a glass of whisky in his hand, shrugged and took another sip.

"Sir," said Poe, "you wrote an entire volume about a fish. A fish."

"And that fish, sir, earned me a Nobel Prize."

Saul sighed. They always seemed to squabble.

"Gentlemen, you're here to give me advice."

"Keep the line, kid," said Hemingway. "You agree don't you, Scott?"

"Sure," said Fitzgerald. He took another sip. That was

all he said that evening.

Saul dismissed them and they faded to nothing. He tried to continue with his work but gave up after a fruitless twenty minutes.

But he had his opening line and the ghosts had seemed to like it. He went to bed happy.

***

The following Saturday, Saul and Kate went out for dinner with his brother and his wife.

Where Saul always dressed a little shabbily, David was sharp and neat. He was six feet tall, where Saul was five feet eleven. That inch made all the difference.

As they were seated at their table, David and Kate exchanged a secret little smile.

"So how's the book going, Saul?" said his brother.

"Oh, not too bad. I've made a start."

He neglected to say that the start consisted of one line. A line about a dead dog.

"And what's it about?" said Jane, his brother's wife, a flawless looking woman in every sense.

It was a question which Saul hated. He didn't really know how to answer it and made his usual vague reply.

"Oh, it's about the human condition, a man who finds redemption," he said.

David and Jane looked at him expectantly.

"When his dog dies," Saul blurted out desperately. "He's drunk and runs him over."

"Well," said David, "it sounds interesting."

Saul hoped the conversation would move on to something else. But Jane didn't let him off the hook.

"Tell me about your hero. The one who runs the dog over. What's he like?"

"Actually," said Saul, "I don't really like going into

detail about work in progress."

To his relief, they drifted onto another topic. But as he ate his starter, Saul realised that he knew nothing about his main character, either physically, spiritually or psychologically.

That evening, after Kate had gone to bed, Saul sat at the kitchen table with an empty notebook and a freshly sharpened pencil in front of him.

"What *is* my main character like?" he said aloud.

They came to him. Four ghosts. They came not one by one, but all together. Three young women and a dismal looking man who sat at the far end of the table, away from the others. They wore Victorian dress and looked familiar but Saul couldn't quite place them.

"If you don't mind me asking, who are you?"

"I'm Currer Bell," said the first.

"I'm Ellis Bell," said the second.

"I'm Acton Bell," said the third.

The young man said nothing, just glowered from the far end of the table.

"Currer, Ellis, Acton," murmured Saul, trying to think where he'd heard the names.

It came to him. "You're the Bronte sisters..." He pointed to the sullen young man. "...and you're Bramwell, the brother."

"We *are* the Bronte sisters. I'm Emily. Now, if you'll take my advice, I would create a strong character like my Heathcliffe. Everybody remembers him."

"Or Mr Rochester, from Jane Eyre," said Currer, evidently Charlotte.

"What about Mr Huntingdon from Tenant of Wildfell Hall?" said Acton.

Emily jerked a thumb in her direction and leaned back on the rear legs of her chair.

"This is Anne. Nobody remembers her. We call her

'the other one', don't we Charlotte? And Mr Huntingdon is a watery sort of fellow. You couldn't compare him to my Heathcliffe."

Charlotte was not as rude as Emily and did not reply.

"Charlotte," said Saul eagerly. "Yes, you wrote Jane Eyre. Mr Rochester and his mad wife. He dies and she says, 'Reader I buried him'."

"Something like that," said Charlotte with a hint of smugness.

The young man raised his hand.

"Can I say something," he said.

"Oh, not now, Bramwell," said Emily. "You're not a writer after all. You're a painter. Or so I'm told. That thing you did of the three of us wasn't too good was it? Couldn't recognise myself, made me look like some kind of goblin."

"What I was going to say," continued Bramwell, "is that I'm not sure the gentleman's hero should run over a dog. Even if he is drunk."

"Well, you should know, brother," said Emily. "And if it isn't the brandy it's the laudanum. And really, if you're going to paint a tree, you should make it look like a tree."

"Well, at least he did more than one painting, dear," said Anne with venom. "How many novels did you write? Just the one as I recall."

"Yes, I was busy being dead. But it's made me immortal."

The four siblings continued to talk, but they descended into mere squabbling and Saul switched on the kettle to make coffee.

"You see," said Emily, "the other one gets a little defensive because she's not as famous as Charlotte and me. Even Bramwell is better known, but that's only because he's seen as the one who just paints bad pictures. A bit like Ringo I suppose."

Saul looked at her. "How do you know about Ringo?"

"Well, we like to keep up."

Saul realised he had gleaned nothing from them. He also realised that the kettle had been boiling for over a minute. He got up and switched it off and poured water into his cup. When he returned to the table, the four of them had gone. All that remained was a little vapour which wound its way around the legs of the chairs.

He returned to his notebook and pencil and made a futile attempt to write about his hero.

To his surprise, a figure began to form. He waited. It was unusual for there to be a second visit. At length he saw him. He wore a long, thick plaid cloak and his wavy hair was white and unkempt. He reminded Saul of his grandmother.

"William McGonagall," said the man without being asked. He was softly spoken with a pleasing Scottish lilt.

"I'm sorry, I don't know your work."

"I am a poet and a tragedian. And I have come to offer you a verse. May I read it?"

"Yes, of course."

McGonagall took a folded parchment from a deep pocket in his jacket. He unfolded it and, with a theatrical gesture of his left hand, read.

"Twas in the year two, nought, one and nine
A four legged beast there was, a most excellent canine
In the gloaming he would bark at dusk without fail
And in daylight hours would commence to wag his silvery tail

Then one dismal day a man returned home less than sober
And carelessly ran his poor dog over

He turned off the motor of his vehicle and heard a brief yelp
Saw what he had done and cried out, good people please help

Could he save the hound, he thought that he could
Then he saw the tarmac, spattered with blood
He knew the dog was beyond the assistance of even the most skilful vet
He tore out his hair and cried out, good heavens, I've just squashed my pet

It wasn't a cat that resembled a mat
But alas and alack, a poor hound that was flat
He buried him with all due reverence 'neath a green holly bush
Because a labradoodle is too big to flush

So to save poor creatures in future, which no man would debunk
We should not return home in motor cars when drunk

McGonagall methodically folded the sheet and returned it to his pocket.

Saul didn't say anything. He *couldn't* say anything, he didn't dare. "Very interesting," he finally managed to say. "But how did you know my main character runs over his dog?"

It was too late. McGonagall had already faded away.

It was only then that Saul realised. Of course he knew his main character had run over his dog. He knew everything about his book. They all did.

***

Saul found progress slow, grindingly slow. Each day he sat at the table and waited while his old laptop booted up.

One evening, he sat alone at the kitchen table, his head in his hands. "Am I wasting my time?" he murmured to himself. "Should I just give up and get my old job back?"

He sniffed the air. "Is that fish?" he thought.

A figure began to form, a strange looking man with a stern looking face and stern clothing, coarse and black and topped by a stovepipe hat. He had a pale face with a beard all the way around his face but no moustache.

Saul thought he looked familiar but couldn't place him.

"Good evening, sir," the man thundered, "Herman Melville at your service. I can see you're finding it difficult to make progress."

"Melville, of course. Could I ask you to lower your voice? My wife is asleep upstairs."

"Of course, sir, of course," whispered Melville. "Now, my advice is this. Persevere, sir, persevere."

"I just can't seem to get started."

"I had the self-same problem with Moby Dick at the beginning."

"Moby Dick? But it's a masterpiece."

"Not to start with. Let me read you the first draft."

Melville took out a few sheaves of paper. He read, loud and strong.

"'Call me, Ishmael,' said Captain Ahab…"

Saul pointed to the ceiling. "My wife, Mr Melville. You don't want to wake her, believe me."

Melville held up his hand in apology. He began again, much more quietly.

"'Call me, Ishmael,' said Captain Ahab, one fist to his mouth another to his ear, mimicking a telephonic device. I liked Captain Ahab. He didn't have me tied to a barrel every Friday evening like the other cabin boys…"

He read a page or so and when he had finished, Saul looked at him aghast. "What was that?" he said.

"My first effort. Then I thought, what this story needs is a big white whale. And that changed everything. The point is however, I persevered."

"I see, I see," said Saul. "Then what should I do?"

"Persevere," said Melville.

Saul waved his hand wearily to dismiss him. Melville disappeared at once. But the smell of fish lingered.

**

Saul continued to write with the sound advice of his literary phantoms. They were many and varied, writers he liked, writers he didn't like and writers he'd never heard of. D H Lawrence gave him advice on love scenes. Marcel Proust gave him advice on how to keep his manuscript short.

Shakespeare did not appear, though his pretenders did. Saul remembered the night. The table was filled with men, and one woman, all purporting to be the man from Stratford.

He recognised Marlowe, who sat brooding in a corner, his arms folded over his chest.

"I'm not Shakespeare," he muttered. "I know I'm not. Never was."

The others, however, announced that they had written the works of the famous bard.

One of them, a plump looking fellow, introduced himself as Edward de Vere, Earl of Oxford. He presented his case. Evidence from life, he said. King Lear had three daughters, *he* had three daughters. Hamlet was captured by pirates, *he* was captured by pirates. Ergo, he wrote Shakespeare's play.

Francis Bacon then presented his evidence, based, he

said, on codes and ciphers.

"I take words from the folio and apply the Bacon coefficient," he said.

"The Bacon coefficient?" said Saul. "You named it after yourself then?"

"No, actually, it's because I thought of it while I was eating breakfast."

"I see. And how does the…Bacon coefficient work?"

Bacon picked a passage, made a quick calculation, and came up with a sentence. '*Shakspur never writ a word of them*'.

"You see?" he said in triumph.

There were other theories too, each more ridiculous than the last. When Saul dismissed the ghosts, all that remained was the faint stink of Elizabethan plumbing.

***

After a few months' endeavour, Saul realised he didn't have a genre, let alone a plot. He tried romantic comedy but disliked his characters and had to kill them off in various and satisfying ways. His cute but independent heroine and square jawed but unconventional hero who was unable to commit, perished together in a terrible farming accident fifteen pages in.

He tried romance but his visit from the ghost of Barbara Cartland sickened him. Her perfume lingered long after he dismissed her.

Science fiction and horror were alien to him but he tried anyway. He thought of mashing them up but his handful of pages of an unconventional werewolf on a moon bound spaceship was as bad as he imagined.

He wrote several chapters of a western. Zane Grey came and advised him to add colour to his characters. He went to revise what he'd written one morning and read.

Tall, flinty but unconventional sheriff Arch Eastmere rode towards the small town. The heat was hot and little rivers of sweat ran down his face. His deputy was a green kid called Jim Brown.

He drank too much cheap whisky, perhaps, but he always got the job done by bucking authority.

He was looking forward to seeing his girl, Violet, in the saloon. As he rode into town he saw his hated enemy, Red Baxter.

"Well, howdy, sheriff," said Baxter.

"I told you to leave town, Baxter."

"Well I didn't. I'm gonna kill you, sheriff and then I'm gonna plug your deputy."

Eastmere was angry.

"You're yellow, Red. And Brown's green. And Violet will be blue if I'm dead."

His face turned white with rage.

Saul shook his head and quickly deleted what he'd written.

He was visited by William McGonagall the next evening, like some kind of chorus of the damned.

"I have been following your progress, sir. I thought I would offer a verse to comment on what you have written thus far."

"Very well," said Saul wearily.

McGonagall took a folded paper from his pocket and, with the usual flourish of his left hand, read.

"There was a man who wrote a novel
I think he would've preferred a garret or hovel
His head is filled with the idea of artistic suffering
Though he spends time idle while his computing device is buffering

He received sound advice from a man called Herman
He lived in New England so wasn't an old German
He read from his book called Moby Dick
It took some time to write because he didn't write quick

He began a colourful tale in the old west
And his sheriff shot Red Baxter, lest
He killed his girl with whom he then became frisky
And afterwards drank a bottle of inexpensive whisky

He folded the paper and replaced it in his pocket with a hint of smugness on his face.

"You see, sir. It's just a way of letting us all know how you're getting on."

"Let who know?" said Saul.

"All of us," his voice dropped to a whisper and he pointed at the ceiling. "Up there."

Saul pointed to the kitchen door to let McGonagall know he was dismissed.

***

He finally settled on a police procedural with a brilliant but unconventional detective. He drinks too much expensive wine but gets the job done by bucking authority.

Agatha Christie and Arthur Conan Doyle duly came to give advice. Instead, they bickered about whose detective was superior until Edgar Poe arrived late and told them his Monsieur Dupin was better than the fat Belgian and the cocaine sniffing fellow from Baker Street.

He wrote steadily, an hour or so at a sitting. When his computer felt too hot he switched it off and did something else until it had cooled sufficiently.

He checked his progress one morning. His writing had gravitas, certainly, but it lacked humour. He'd resisted the obvious comedy relief but it now felt too serious.

Saul wasn't a naturally funny man and found it difficult to inject even the most insipid comedy into his story.

"I don't even know what comedy is," he said gloomily.

An odd looking figure materialised at the table. He was deathly white, like a marble statue. Saul had no idea who he was.

"Comedy," said the man with an accent thickly Mediterranean, "could be described as tragedy plus time."

"I don't understand, Mr…"

"Aeschylus."

"Sorry, Mr Aeschylus."

"It's just Aeschylus. I was the foremost writer of tragedies on the ancient Greek stage. Not that Sophocles would agree with that. But then he wrote strange stuff about a man who has a mother he'd like to…"

"Sorry," interrupted Saul, "but what were you saying about tragedy plus time."

"Well, take my case. Did you know that eagles in ancient Greece used to drop turtles onto the rocks below to break their shells?"

"No," said Saul, wondering what this had to do with comedy.

"Well, I was walking along one day when a turtle fell onto my head. Killed me. An eagle mistook my bald head for a rock, you see. Now, it wasn't funny at the time, but tell me it's not funny now."

"Hilarious," said Saul and dismissed the unfortunate Greek. Aeschylus' maniacal laughter lingered for a few moments.

Saul dismissed the idea of inserting comedy and pressed on with his story.

As he sat at the table the next evening, McGonagall came once more.

"May I?" he said, reaching into his coat pocket.

"Of course," said Saul wearily.

McGonagall read with his usual theatrical fervour.

"If your story reads rather dull
Add a few gags about a man with a cracked skull
Or put in a line about boiling a bunny
There's bound to be somebody who finds it funny

It's different strokes for different folks
You just don't know if anybody will laugh at your jokes
Forget the comedy, do yourself a favour
After all, people used to laugh at Love Thy Neighbour."

He was about to deliver the next verse when Saul held up his hand to stop him.

"Thank you, Mr McGonagall," he said rudely. He then dismissed the poet with a curt wave of his hand.

***

It took him about nine months but one fine day he added the last full stop. His novel was finished. Exhausted, he drank a small glass of whisky to celebrate.

Nine months. He hadn't been aware of his wife's resentment in that time and certainly hadn't been aware that she was having an affair with his brother.

After a few hours editing the manuscript he sent it to publishers. Many, many publishers. All his submissions were sent online, except one which was sent by mail.

Then he waited. Waited each day, checking his emails

every five minutes.

Nothing arrived until the third week. It was a rejection, short and terse.

"With regret, your novel does not meet our requirements."

The next day he received his second rejection.

"It is with *great* regret that your novel does not *quite* meet our *current* requirements."

That was more promising, thought Saul. Those two adjectives and one adverb made all the difference.

After that, the rejections came in an electronic torrent, two or more each day until his list of publishers was exhausted. It was the bitterest of pills to swallow. As he sat at the kitchen table, he regretted that last full stop. Had he never written his novel he could have clung to the notion that he would do so in the future. He would be an aspiring writer, not a failed writer.

He heard the morning's mail fall onto the carpet.

"Christ, more overdue bills," he muttered.

He picked up the envelopes, the usual junk mail and urgent looking, red liveried demands for payment.

One envelope stood out though. He recognised the name franked on the top right. It was the publisher to whom he'd mailed his manuscript. He slit the envelope neatly with a sharp knife and read the letter. To his amazement it was an offer to publish his book. He read the letter and then read it again with increasing elation. Then he saw a footnote which made his heart sink. To have his book published, it said, would cost him four thousand pounds plus VAT.

For the rest of the day, he wrestled with the problem. Finally he rationalised any objections away and told himself it could be a good investment. He posted the completed form and cheque just before his wife returned from work.

As part of the deal he received two free copies of his novel. He read it, the first time he'd read it in full since finishing it. It wasn't truly awful. That would have been preferable somehow. Instead, it was merely lukewarm, tepid, insipid, clichéd and utterly worthless.

**

Six months later a familiar looking envelope dropped through the door. Saul hid it beneath the others and joined his wife for breakfast. She saw the corner poking out.

"Is that another royalty cheque?" she said.

"Hmm? Is it? Oh yes."

"Open it," she said.

He slit open the envelope and fished out the handwritten cheque.

"How much?" said Kate.

"Two pounds forty three," he said miserably.

"How much is that in total then?"

"Not sure. About forty three pounds I suppose."

Kate tried not to laugh. She knew about the publisher and she knew about the cheque for four thousand pounds plus VAT. To be fair, though, she didn't rub it in.

Saul realised that even though he'd got his job back and all the overdue bills were paid, he hadn't achieved closure.

While his wife slept that night, he crept downstairs and sat at the kitchen table. He waited. It didn't take long. McGonagall duly appeared.

"Read it," said Saul, without being asked.

McGonagall took out a few sheets of paper and, with his usual dramatic gestures, read.

"I sing tonight of a bookish man
Who wrote a novel with great elan
After many false starts he wrote of a crime
Which had baffled the police for a very long time

While many of us offered him advice at home
The writer pressed on and finished his tome
He sent it to publishers with high hopes
But all he received was a long string of nopes

So he had his book published for a sum of money
His wife found out and didn't think it was funny
She was angry he'd wasted ninety six thousand bob
He had no choice but to return to his old job

So I warn you now, you writers of wit
Don't write a book that's completely mediocre

McGonagall handed the sheet to Saul. "For you," he said. "My final gift."

"Well, goodbye, Mr McGonagall. And thank you."

Saul watched as the poet began to slowly fade. Just before he disappeared, he turned.

"Just one last thing, sir. I really don't think you should have killed the dog…"

FRANCOPHONE

Hazel McLoughlin

Since the day and hour Mlle Thomas had walked into his class at the Secondary School, Michael O'Rourke had been a fan of French. She'd only stayed the one term, but it was enough to infatuate half the school and for Michael to identify an obsession. And whereas Father O'Sullivan, the anti-climactic replacement for the tres belle Mademoiselle, who had learned his French at a seminary in Angers, did little to develop the Francophile in Michael, or indeed anyone else in his class, the notion to speak French persisted.

It took a sideways step when his Leaving Cert. results meant he was lucky to get a start as a trainee mechanic in a garage in Tallaght, owned by a cousin of his father. It had taken a night in Mulligans with the lads after a rugby international against Allez la France to rekindle his linguistic ambition.

He enrolled in a French evening class in Ballyfermot. His teacher, a stout Madame from Nantes drilled them like a sergeant-major and soon he could je m'appelle and j'ai trois frères et deux soeurs with the rest of the class.

The other lads in the garage thought he was a feckin' eejit to be spending his money and time on such a gimp of an activity. If they'd known the word, they might even have called it bourgeois.

They were all in Mulligans. Seamus was after getting himself engaged to Dympna McCarthy and was taking the opportunity to celebrate without her, while he still could. Pints of the dark stuff were flowing like Liffey water and the craic was grand. Michael had no recollection of getting home but he woke up in his bed-sit in Clondalkin in a rancid muddle of sheets, still wearing his coat and his trainers on the wrong feet.

"Merde!" he thought "Quelle heure est-il? Et merde encore. Il faut me depecher pour aller au boulot." It was only when he was helping himself to une goutte d'eau straight from the tap to quench the fierce thirst - un soif feroce in his throat, that he realized he was talking to himself in French.

He was half an hour en retard arriving at the garage and had to endure a bollicking from the boss, cousin of his dad or not. "Desole," he said and got another bollicking a cause de prendre la pisse.

You'd have been taking a risk lighting a match anywhere near the collective fug of hangover that hung over the lads this morning, reducing their normal banter to a more animalistic series of grunts and sighs. It was the lunch-break before any of them recovered the power of speech.

"Bejay, ye were rightly scuttered last night," said Seamus.

"Je le sais," replied Michael, "Que j'ai une sacree guele de bois!"

"What are ye after saying?"

"Je ne sais pas si je suis encore dechire."

"Are ye langered still or just messin? Here, lads, would yis listen to Michael. He's after losing the power of common speech. Will we take him to the A and E at St Vincent's?"

"Mais non! Ca n'est pas necessaire," said Michael, finding himself waving his arms with Gallic emphasis.

For the rest of the afternoon, a wary distance grew between him and the other mechanics. They had no idea how to handle the situation and Michael himself was no help. So, at the end of the day, the universal panacea prevailed.

"So are ye coming for a jar?"

"Ca m'est egal!" answered Michael and no-one was any the wiser.

They all met in Mulligans, as usual. And, as usual, the lads ordered their stout.

"Pour moi, un vin rouge," said Michael to the barman, who raised a shaggy eyebrow in surprise but was sufficiently au fait with any drink containing alcohol to understand the order.

"What ails him this evening?" he said to Michael's friends.

"Ah, hasn't he a frog in his throat," said Anto, the wit, though the humour of the witticism dwindled with its regular repetition throughout the evening.

Having drunk his red wine as a volumetric match to the lads' pints, Michael was more than un peu pompette by closing time. And the windy draught of fresh air blowing up the quays proved to be the coup de grace. He lay untidily on a bench by the side of the Liffey.

When he opened his eyes, Mlle Thomas, in all her gorgeousness, was standing beside him.

"Leve-toi, Michael," she coaxed. "Tu ne peux pas rester ici. Les flics…"

Behind her head, like a halo, he noticed the bright blue light, turning dizzily on the bridge. Michael's head began to turn dizzily too and the last words he heard himself slur before the alcoholic mists drew the curtain on his consciousness were "Au revoir, Mlle."

The two guards shuffled the inert body into the back of the patrol car.

"Bluthered blind he is" said one to the other "And jabberin' away in some foreign language."

For an entire week, not a drop crossed his lips. Getting

banjoed every night wouldn't keep him in a job and Michael wasn't sure he liked the way the drink was playing tricks with his mind.

The next time he went to his French evening class and Mme Berteuil asked "Vous etes de quelle nationalite?" he was content to answer, with enough of a Dublin jackeen accent to validate the reply, "Je suis irlandais."

Sure one of these fine days he'd be speaking it fluently.

ONE NIGHT IN BANGOR

Ian Collier

King's Gambit pawn to e4– let's see how he's thinking–
ah classic response.
French defence, keeping options open.

Push on, he's fingering his tower, always watch for
tells, he's looking to castle early on.

No! Change of direction, or maybe me falling for
misdirection- tilting at windmills.

But tilting at windmills can have payoffs too- that's
where I met Emma.

***

"You been dragged here too? You look almost as bored
as I am"

"I can't even get a decent 4G signal here. I'm
Emmeline. You can call me Emma. Been here long?"

"Murray. Dad was a fan of *Groundhog Day*, before
you ask. I'm not sure how long- officially two days, but I
swear it was 2021 when we set off and we seem to have
arrived in like 1920."

"We got in late last night; Mum's partner wants to
work through Trip Advisor's list of *Things to do on
Anglesey* starting at 16 and working up. What we do
tomorrow is anyone's guess."

"You have something to look forwards to Emma. The
restaurants open up on Wednesday!"

"What do you mean Murray?"

"Ah- I guess you ate on the mainland last night? It seems like all the eating places close on Monday and today. We spent an hour last night trying pubs. In the end, we got pizzas from the Coop in the place with the long name. Mum was sooooooo pissed, she'd sworn she wasn't going to do any cooking."

"Did you look at the windmill?"

"Yeah, it's certainly a windmill, Mum and her partner went off around to Iron Age village-I've had enough living in the past. I saw you in there, you didn't see me? You stepped aside to let me up the ladder."

"Yeah, I saw you, you were the only thing in there worth looking at."

OK it was a yucky line, but she smiled and I felt I'd not gone too far - unlike his bishop. I figured even if I overdid it, it wasn't like we'd ever meet again anyway-WRONG!

Now, if I use my knight, it's covered by my bishop so he can risk his queen if he likes, but it will be a blood bath with me sinking his battle ship.

DAMN! I was too timid, I should have used my bishop. That way I'd threaten his queen as a bonus. He's back to tapping his rook.

***

Next morning Mum had a real arse on her. A week away for the first time in two years and she has to cook for two consecutive nights- she was really not happy. Dad making breakfast didn't calm her down. I went down to the nature reserve behind to cottages to get out' the way. Saw a huge black crow on the carcass of a calf. I guess that's nature "red in tooth and claw … and beak" as our Biology teacher doesn't quite say. It was in a wooded dip, felt a bit like a tunnel – probably a river when it's winter.

Got back to the cottages and across the, like square, the 6 cottages were set around, I saw her again- they were getting into an Audi A4, a red one. Emma's mum's boyfriend was standing beside the driver's door and looking daggers at her. I wondered if he'd had to cook last night too.

As she glanced over at me, I realised my mouth was gaping. She pivoted from a sulky pout to a shy giggle then looked away getting into the back of the car. The boy sat beside her must have said something causing her to punch him in the shoulder. I didn't hear it, but I could see their mum telling them that if they didn't behave all hell would break loose. If it broke loose on this god-forsaken island it would feel at home briefly until it died of boredom. They drove off with her looking back at me and smiling, I went crimson and headed into our cottage.

There I made a dash for the bathroom- I wasn't having them see me looking like that.

"Come on Murray we've been waiting you know – the Transport Museum will be closed in a couple of hours. And I'm like- "You think there's going to be things there that will take a couple of hours to see?"

I was right- if Dad hadn't got all sloppy about some car that Grandad had back in the day we'd have been around in 30 minutes. There were some cool military vehicles, but overall it was very meh. Then we went further along that road to the coast. Huge car park, but we still had to do four laps of it before finding a space, then joined the pilgrimage to the beach. I noticed six red Audis during our jaunts around the car park. On the beach I went on walks, alone, in each direction while Mum and Dad sat watching the sea, but no sign of her, or her family.

I checked the *Things to do on Anglesey* list I guess they must have done the quarry yesterday too. Depending how long they spent trudging around they may have finished off the list- or just given up for the day. By today? Probably given up and gone to the mainland.

***

Back at the cottages I sat outside playing against Bobby Fischer – ok he wasn't actually there- just a chess app on my mobile, but I jumped into one of his games when he was two pawns down and tried to think how to beat him and tried even harder not to repeat the mistakes Lubynik had made in the 70s. Before Fischer could crush me, their car turned up. She and her brother had clearly not got on any better after being given the warning that morning. She slammed the car door announcing that she was going for a walk and headed off down the hill towards the nature reserve. Mum's boyfriend shouted to be back by 7. I had just under an hour and also the dilemma of how long I could decently wait before heading after her: too soon would be very uncool, too long would mean I wasn't interested. Then another thought hit me. If she got out of view I wouldn't know which of the paths she'd taken. There's loads branching and crossing each other- it would be like finding an eagle in a haystack. Now there's a stupid saying, but hey maybe eagles nest in haystacks? I closed the game and headed off- just seeing her take a turn into the start of the woods- almost running, while I thought she wasn't looking, but then as I got near that path she stepped out from behind a tree. I went from dash to saunter and tried to slow my breathing down- not cool talking to a girl when panting- she'd think I was a sex-pest or somethink.

"Hey Murray," she said. She was like, so cool and natural.

"Hey Emma- that your brother in the car?"

"Step brother- he's such a dork, but everyone seems to think he's it. I really hate him at times."

"Must be awful. What's so special about him?"

"Well he's doing his A levels so he gets out of any trips he doesn't fancy for one thing."

"That where he was yesterday?"

"Hey- you're as bad as half my friends always asking about him."

"Sorry. Where'd you go today?"

"Hollyhead and a lighthouse. Mum got all nostalgic when she saw a Woolworths with the sign still up over the back door. She dragged us all around the front- it's a closed down Poundland now. Have you been up to the Lighthouse yet?"

"Not yet. Any good?"

"It's worse than PE with all the steps up and down, and it stinks of bird poo- but there's like some remains nearby of stone age houses. Half buried like Hobbit holes."

"Cool- I expect we'll go there. I'll try to see them- I love the old films like LOTR. I know Dad said we're going to Beaumaris tomorrow. He thinks it's a major place, with a castle and pier and shops- like a real city, and I'm like, 'Look at the map Dad- it's smaller than the country park near home'. And he's like- 'Everything is relative.' Like duh!"

It seemed like seconds later, but must have been most of an hour, our chatting was interrupted when there's a shout from the cottages for someone called Charlie.

She leans up from the tree- "That's 'Dad.' " And she gives the word air quotes.

"Charlie?"

"Yeah- Charlotte is my official name, but I wanted to be named after one of the suffragettes."

Before we could say more, they pinged her phone and

she left- saying she'd be down at the same spot tomorrow at the same time if she could.

I'd pulled!

***

He's playing with that castle again- yep there it goes, I knew he'd get there in the end, what a good boy he is, now, to move my knight that's been sat waiting so long he'd forgotten about it.

Beaumaris was living down to my expectations. Up and down the high street, along the sea front and the pier, not a slot machine in sight; the only reels were on fishing rods. On the land end of the pier there's a fenced off play area, fairground rides for little kids, trampolines, and a big chess set. There were a couple of kids playing with it and while Mum and Dad went to the car to eat their chips, I hung back and watched. The older one at least knew what went in which direction, so I gave the younger one some tips. Then I became aware of a hand dipping into my chips. I snatched the bag away and was mid-expletive when I realised it was Emma- I should have known from the blue nail varnish.

And she's like, "Hey- don't be such a greedy pig."

I offered her the bag apologising that I'd not clocked it was her.

She started giving advice to the older boy and they got fed up of us interfering and left for the corkscrew slide.

"Fancy a game? I'll pay," I asked.

"Yeah sure."

I treated it like speed chess, not really thinking more than move ahead, and she wasn't doing badly. Then her stepbrother occupied exactly the position we'd been at earlier, leaning on the wooden fence, and he started giving her advice. Some of it she took, and some she didn't, and suddenly I found myself having to think as my bishops both left the board in quick succession. We reached a stalemate, and he said it was time to go, but before she left we hooked up on Facebook, since that was fastest she reckoned.

Great- got him- from here on all he can do is look for the least bad choices- checkmate in 3 or lose his queen. There goes the battleship! He responds with bishop takes knight, but he's missed that it leaves his rook uncovered, and... check! All he can do is run away. Again his only options are bad ones.

We managed to get another evening together down in the woods, but that was the last time I saw her, up to now, here in Bangor, at the UK under 18 Chess Championships. There she is standing behind her stepbrother and I am really struggling to read her expression. Is she happy for me to crush him? Will she take it personally? My head is like, flip-flopping between focusing on the game and focusing on the girl.

And then she smiles and winks.

COLD WHITE HORSE

Mark Kockelbergh

Death doesn't ride on a cold white horse
But a bicycle made for two
He sits at the front, jingles the bell
And leaves the back seat free, for me. Or you.

In a blue pinstripe suit, shiny black shoes
And a bowler hat perched on his head
He rides through the town and sums us all up
In his books of the quick and the dead

He flirts with your guardian angel
Then tells her, 'I'm sorry for your loss'.
Sometime they laugh and just flip a coin
But we still look both ways when we cross

One day he might tap on your shoulder
A face with no anger or pity
You ask him, 'Why me?' He says, 'Why not?'
And together you ride from the city

ENCOUNTERS

Chris Allen

There is a tale that, roundabout 1930, in Robinsonville, Mississippi, a young black man with a love of the blues ventured into a juke joint where he had a notion to try his luck and get noticed. The place was heaving with folks because, as the young man very well knew, two legends of the Delta blues were on stage doing their stuff. Now, as the musicians stepped out between sets, in order to apply a little deep south lubrication to their throats, that young man stepped right up on that stage, picked up a guitar and gave the crowd a taste of his own playing. Well, down in the delta, folks surely know what they like and what they don't and they ain't too shy about telling you straight, so them boys in the bar told that young man straight enough.

"Hey, boy, you be just noising us, you know that? That the best you can do?"

Afore too long they told the juke owners straight enough too.

"Why don't some of y'all go down and make that boy put that thing down, he running us crazy!"

So, like any right-minded folk, the owners took the young man off of the stage, tossed him out into the night and that was the end of that.

Except it wasn't, cos that young man, he had sass, and he wasn't gonna give up so easy, so, he squared his shoulders and strode off along the road. After a while he came to a crossroads, lonesome in the Mississippi darkness, where a figure waited, blacker than the Delta night. Well, the young man and the figure they had themselves a right long conversation, negotiations were had, terms agreed and then they both walked away, each of them pleased with the business they had done.

For 12 months, nobody saw sight nor sound of the young black guitar player but one hot, humid evening that boy showed up, bold as brass, at another juke joint, in Banks, Mississippi, and walked straight up onto the stage. For a moment the whole place fell silent as the sea of faces looked up in expectation and then the young man hit the first note out of the battered guitar and the folks there was hit with a wave of blues like nothin' they had ever heard before.

Well, that young man's name was Robert Johnson, and the black figure had many names to many folks, Old Nick, Slewfoot, but, to the people of the Delta, he was Legba, and he gave young Bob the gift of music as his part of the deal.

Such is the legend that has been told and retold, from the smoky blues bars of Chicago and the black communities of the South to the hip joints of New York and beyond. Where the truth lies, no-one rightly knows but, for me, there is a sense of fitness in the thought that the Devil's music was taught to that young man by the Devil himself.

***

Nathan Turner played guitar, liked the Blues but he was to meet the Devil far more prosaically in a community centre in the English Midlands.

The guitar group was finishing up for the evening. Nathan carefully slid his guitar into the gig bag and looked around him at the other members. Rich was chatting to Len, neither of them seeming to be in any rush to pack up their instruments as they discussed what they had played over the last two hours. Nathan liked Rich, a big amiable guy who had the enviable ability to put anyone at their ease and just loved his music. Len was ok but was a purist and had strong opinions about the Blues which he did not mind sharing at any opportunity. A lean, stringy man, he was holding forth again to Rich.

"It's like I keep saying, if you want to play Blues, the only way is acoustic. As soon as you go electric you lose the meaning, man, do you get it?"

Nathan watched as Rich made some diplomatic comment and led the conversation into safer waters.

"I see Len is pontificating again," Angie Bartlett said in her vinegar voice, looking at Nathan expectantly as if she thought it his duty to agree with her and add his own criticisms to hers.

"He's alright," Nathan replied, "He's just passionate about things." Nathan did not understand why Angie actually kept coming to the group considering that, every week, she disagreed with the song choices, complained about the inferior quality of the other player's instruments and was generally negative about everything and everyone. Angie snorted derisively and wandered back over to where she had left Tom, who was the group leader and organiser.

"You should say something, Tom, it's getting beyond a joke."

Tom chose to ignore her without appearing to and addressed the rest of the group who were now all packed up and heading towards the exit.

"Thanks for tonight, guys, everyone did great. See you all next week. Any one fancy a quick one at the Saracen?"

There were a few replies in the affirmative to this suggestion, as always.

Nathan slung his gig bag over his shoulder and began to make his way across the room to the door.

"Hi Nathan, are you going for a drink?" Cathy appeared alongside him, fastening her coat up.

"No," he replied "I'm going straight off tonight. Got to catch the bus back."

He flicked the light switches off and held the door open for her.

Speaking to Cathy always made Nathan feel slightly awkward. She had joined the group a few weeks ago and was pretty good on the old vintage Hofner Senator that she had brought along. She was young, early twenties Nathan guessed, with a shock of curly black hair that hung to her shoulders and framed an oval face which had a frank, open expression. Cathy looked up at him as they passed through the door and out into the car park where the stars shone crisply in the October night sky.

"How come you always go straight off, Nathan?" she asked, pulling her coat collar and big multi coloured scarf more tightly around her neck against the cold.

"Wow, sorry, I didn't mean to be rude." A mortified expression crossed her face. "Big mouth runs away before the brain engages. It's none of my business."

"No, it's fine," Nathan said, "No offence taken." He paused and glanced across at her, noting, not for the first time, the way she moved and how nicely her jeans fitted against her. Raising his eyes, he saw Cathy looking directly at him, obviously aware of his scrutiny. Abashed, he reddened and continued,

"It's just that, well, Emma gets edgy when she's at home too long by herself at night. Not that, you understand, she minds me doing the whole guitar thing, she just doesn't like being alone."

He slung his gig bag higher on his back and hunched his shoulders against the cold as they walked along the path down towards where the bus shelter stood in a pool of light by the streetlamp.

They strode in silence for a few yards, each not sure how to take the conversation forwards until Cathy touched him lightly on the arm.

"Yeah, I get that, Nathan." she said. "Look, forget I ever asked."

Arriving at the bus shelter, they stopped.

"Well, this is me, I guess." He looked over to her hesitantly and, once again she touched his arm, this time the contact registering like a crackle of electricity, even through the thick fabric of his coat.

"Look, Nathan, I think you're quite cool, really." She flashed him a smile and turned away before looking back over her shoulder, "See you next week."

Nathan watched her as she walked on, the big guitar bag on her back making her slim figure look even more diminutive, until she turned the corner and disappeared.

He looked down at the spot on his sleeve where she had touched him, then thrust his hands into his pockets for warmth and settled down to wait for the bus.

He opened the gate and walked up the path to the front door. Blowing on his fingers to warm them, he searched his pocket for the key, opened the door and stepped through into the hallway.

"Hi, I'm back," he called as he unshouldered his bag in the small front study.

There was no reply. Nathan frowned slightly and went through to the lounge.

Emma was sitting in the armchair, wrapped in her dressing gown with her laptop on her knees. She glanced up as Nathan entered and then continued typing.

"It was a good session tonight," he ventured, "What have you been up to?"

Emma looked up again, pausing the keyboard strokes,

and the look, so familiar to Nathan, came over her face.

"Actually, Nat, I've spent the evening trying to make things a little better in the world."

"Well, so have I, in my own way," he replied lightly, "We brought in a little music."

"Great," Emma's voice sharpened almost imperceptibly, but Nathan registered the change, nonetheless, "So while you and your mates have been strumming along together, some of us are getting involved in really important stuff."

Ah, this would be the climate change thing thought Nat. Emma was, in imaginary quotation marks, 'thoroughly committed' to the cause. He decided it would be politic to offer an olive branch.

"Is this the direct-action blog you're working on? Have you managed to increase the likes?"

Emma regarded him, slightly mollified, but unwilling to let him off the hook completely.

"Yes, we're up to a thousand plus followers, now, and Jenny and Mick have given some brilliant input about how we can really make the Government sit up and take notice."

Nathan figured that the coast was probably clear now. He walked around behind her chair and leaned over her resting his hands on her shoulders while he studied at the laptop screen.

"Looks good" he said, "Speaking of which," he let one hand slide down inside the dressing gown, "So do you." His hand slid inside the pyjama top. "How about we go upstairs?"

"Christ, Nat!" Emma yanked his hands away. "You're such a bloody idiot! You really don't understand about any of this, do you? Just piss off and leave me alone!"

She slapped the lid of the laptop shut and stalked across the room to the kitchen door where she turned to him, anger and self-righteousness written across her face.

"Jesus, why I am I wasting my time with a complete tool like you?" She slammed the door and silence fell over the living room. Nathan sighed and slowly made his way upstairs.

***

The session the following week began promisingly enough. Cathy had seated herself next to Nathan when they sat down. She placed the Hofner across her knee and began tuning it, her fingers playing easily across the fretboard as she tried each string in turn and then let loose a fluid scale run to double check. Nathan was acutely aware of her presence and, as ever could not help taking the opportunity to look across at her. Finishing the tuning, she stretched, and the warm breath of her perfume drifted over to him.

"So, how did it go when you got home last week?" she asked.

"Er, yeah, fine," Nat stammered slightly. He pulled a wry face. "Well, if I'm honest, fineish, or even, not very fine, really."

"Oh, sorry to hear that." A shadow of concern crossed her face and then she brightened. "Well, at least you're back here again," again the quick touch on the arm, "and I'm glad to see you."

They ran through two or three numbers to warm up everyone and then Rich suggested that they have a go at "Jumpin' Jack Flash". Tom rifled through his bag and eventually found some sheet music which he passed around.

"Okay, Nathan, Rich, me and Angie will do rhythm, Len, Sue and Cathy, you take turns at lead after each chorus."

They ran through the first time, Len producing his usual competent lead, and on the second run, Cathy began her lead riff.

"No, I'm sorry Cathy, that's not right at all. You're out of tune and off time as well."

Angie had stopped playing and stood in the centre of the group.

"I thought it was ok." Cathy's face registered surprise and hurt.

"Sounded ok to me." Nat said quietly.

There was a low chorus of agreement.

"Well, Tom, what do you think?" Angie had no intention of giving in gracefully.

"We're all learning here," Tom said diplomatically "Come on guys, perhaps we better try something else."

The group moved on.

As they were packing up at the end of the evening, Cathy came over to Nathan.

"Thanks for sticking up for me. I really appreciate it."

Nathan blushed slightly. "Well, there was nothing wrong with your playing," he replied, "She just hates anyone else getting any attention."

Cathy shrugged and then a grin lit up her face. "Well, I guess it takes all sorts. Come on, let's forget about it."

Once again, they were both the last to leave. As they walked across the car park towards the gate Cathy asked innocently,

"So, are you going straight home again, tonight?"

Nathan hesitated before replying, "I'm not sure. Yes, I suppose I should get straight off."

If Cathy was disappointed, she did not show it.

"Ok, Nathan, sir", she said brightly, "In that case, the least I can do is escort you to the bus stop." She held out a crooked arm. "Come on, it's fine. I don't bite."

He stood, slightly nonplussed at the turn of events and

then, grinned in turn and slid his arm through hers.

They walked in a companionable silence along the road, their breath clouding in the cold air, until they reached the bus stop.

"So, I guess this is you." Cathy stood facing him and then, as if on a sudden impulse, reached up and kissed him on the lips. She stepped back and studied his face as if wondering if she had made a mistake. Whatever she saw there seemed to reassure her and, once again, she kissed him, this time, long and slow, pulling his body against hers.

"Nat, don't go back to her," she breathed the words softly to him, "Come home with me tonight, please."

Nathan let his hand caress the side of her face and he gently smiled his acceptance. As he bent to kiss her again, his attention was struck by the fact that, deep down in the back of her green-black eyes, there was a hint of a twinkle of the devil.

THE THEATRE VISIT

Jean Busby

"You will enjoy this play darling," said Jane, taking my hand in hers as we sat down on the front row in the Royal Shakespeare Theatre, Stratford. I was dreading sitting for over two hours trying to understand, "The Tempest," having once nodded off to sleep during another boring play. And would you believe a man with beard sat with his beau also on the front row. He bumped into me in the bar causing me to spill my drink without as much as an apology.

I've never really understood the language of Shakespeare, so you can imagine when the lights are dimmed me trying to understand the play and falling asleep. Although there is plenty of action give me "Star Wars," any day. I can't wait for the interval.

My girl is really enjoying this play, we've only been together for six weeks and I'm so in love with her although we're complete opposites. Jane has a first class honours degree in Chemistry. I've always been attracted to intellectual women. At present I'm just a simple sales assistant selling mobile phones. I haven't mentioned yet that I've decided to set up my own business selling Industrial Cleaning products.

"John Jones," my teacher used to say. "All you seem to do all day is talk. You'll never be able to hold a responsible job down." But I'll prove him wrong when I make my first million.

Hooray, I've managed to keep awake and we're making our way to the bar. Our drinks are pre-ordered.

Unfortunately, trying to enjoy our drinks Beardie Head stands near to us. He is annoying everyone in the bar as his voice is becoming louder and his girlfriend is embarrassed as she tries to look the other way as he downs his pint of beer, followed by a whiskey chaser.

The announcer says that the second half of "The Tempest," will begin in five minutes time. Jane holds my hand and smiles as we walk towards the auditorium. She has beautiful brown eyes. I notice that some people are missing from their seats. Perhaps they have given up the ghost like myself or perhaps they were there for the experience of visiting the famous theatre.

Towards the end of the play, just before the lights come on, to my amusement Beardie Head has fallen asleep and his girlfriend is nudging him to wake up. At least I managed to stay awake. Jane thinks that I'm enjoying the play as I train my eyes to stare into space to avoid them closing.

Well, this will be the first and last Shakespeare play that I'll ever watch but I respect Jane and will not pass any opinion as I don't want to spoil the evening. I have a nice surprise waiting for her when we arrive at the Hilton hotel. There's a bottle of champagne and an engagement ring tucked away in a box of chocolates. And later on we'll watch "Fifty Shades of Grey," then after that "Star Wars."

THE RAIN

Chris Allen

The Rain Falls

Summer rain, boiling off sun-baked asphalt,
Heavy with scented memories that, like some
Vaporous narcotic charm, snatch me from
My world of tedious necessity and cast me
Back through ten thousand thousand dream days,
Each one a fine tapestry, woven with golden lies,
To heal my aching soul.

The Rain Falls

Flanders rain, beating down the head of the child-man
soldier.
He waits, a lice ridden joint of His Majesty's
Uniformed meat, for his mother to come.
For surely she will save him from this savage,
Nightmare circus of mud and death
Where shopkeepers and smiling clerks each
Hack the other down and spill their guts in
Bloody token of their futile patriotism.
But he sits alone in his open grave,
His friends cold and silent around him,
And weeps beneath the leaden skies for all eternity.

The Rain Falls

November rain, chill and relentless against my window.
I look out over the ranks of distant houses,
The winter locked tight within me,
And wonder if I can ever be whole.
I would take a bright flower and, with
Exquisite care, extract and distil its very essence
To drink, to warm my heart;
That ragged part of me that bleeds in the long nights
And dies in the grey dawn.

Still, the Rain Falls

ETERNAL NIGHT

Tony Rattigan

This story was originally published in Diverse Voices *at* Christmas *in 2014, well before the pandemic. (Who knew I was psychic?) It's reprinted here as since then I've written a sequel to it,* Rising Dawn *which follows on from it.*

The old man stood on his porch looking out at the clear, winter, night sky. He sipped a glass of fifty-year-old, malt whisky. He knew it was fifty years old as he had bought it himself when it was new. The whisky was beginning to have an effect on him, it would make him drunk eventually if he had enough but that was all right, there would be no accompanying hangover next morning. He never got hangovers, or colds or indeed any sort of physical ailment. He was immortal after all. That was his blessing and also his curse.

The man pulled his fur-lined cloak tighter around himself, being immortal didn't stop you from feeling the cold. He was feeling melancholy; he always did at this time of year, as the old anniversary approached. Swigging back the rest of his drink he put the glass down carefully. *A turn around the compound might clear my head,* he thought. His boots crunched through the deep snow as he made his night-time patrol.

His first stop was the barn. It was empty now but it still smelt strongly of his animals. No, they were more than just his animals, they were his friends. He had named them all individually and they had become famous. Songs had been sung and stories had been told about them. But they were all gone now, dead and gone, just like everything else. He had taken them out into the world and maybe they had brought back the infection that killed them. They were buried now, out on the plains that they had loved to roam so much.

His next stop was the dormitory. He paused to light a lamp as he entered, the light revealed the empty beds, all neatly made up, as his workers had tidied up before they left for home. A tear came to his eye and a lump to his throat as he remembered his farewells to them all; as they left to spend their last few days with their people back home.

Nobody really knew where the plague had come from. Was it some man-made horror, accidentally released from a secret laboratory, or was it some natural disease like Swine Flu or Foot and Mouth? What difference did it make now? The damage had been done, what was served by pointing the finger at any one person or group or state or even Mother Nature? Gone is gone.

When the news of the outbreak had first started to filter through to them, the old man had ventured out into the world to see for himself what was going on. But later as the plague spread throughout the globe he'd stopped his visits for fear of contamination. Hopefully their remote location would protect them from harm. After all, something here had made him immortal; perhaps it would reach out to cover his workers. At least, that's what he'd hoped.

Alas it was not to be. At first it was just the reindeer that showed signs of the disease. Maybe they had brought back the infection from their recent journeys into the world. One by one they faltered and died. He'd prayed that perhaps it would only take them and leave the higher beings, with more developed immune systems, alone. But his workers too, soon fell foul of the spreading plague. Everyone, except the old man whom no illness could touch.

When it became apparent that not even the remoteness of the North Pole could save them, his Elves had come to him and asked to be released as they wished to return to their families, who lived deep in the woods of the Scandinavian countries, where they were hidden from Man. If they were going to die, they said, they wanted to be surrounded by their clans, in the homes of their ancestors. So they had left, leaving him alone.

The man wandered through the dormitory and into the workshop where the toys had been made. He gazed on all the toys that had been left uncompleted or stacked in the corner, finished and just waiting to be packed. He thought of all the generations that he had given toys to, who had gone on to grow up and have children of their own. He had brought them toys every Christmas. And now they were all gone. There would be no more Christmases, no more toys, no more Mankind.

Father Christmas dropped to his knees and sobbed, *'The children! Couldn't you have spared the children?'* he cried out to the cold, unfeeling Universe. And the last living being on Earth, who would live alone forever, wept for all the children that were no more and would never be again.

RISING DAWN

Tony Rattigan

The old man took one last look around the compound. He'd packed his tools, extra clothing and what food he had left in a small sled that he could tow behind him. He had wondered if he should set fire to the buildings but decided against it, let it remain as a monument to his friends and the animals that had died there, from the plague. Perhaps one day some other creatures could benefit from it, space aliens perhaps? He liked to think so and grinned at the thought. Picking up the harness he settled it on his shoulders and set off, dragging the sled behind him, heading south.

Several centuries had passed since the plague had wiped everyone out and Nick (he no longer thought of himself as Father Christmas, just Nick) decided to go out into the world again and see how it had developed without man's influence. After a few hundred years he hoped that all the unpleasantness would have dissipated, time having reduced the bodies to dust.

Nick travelled down through Canada and headed into Alaska where he crossed the Bering Strait into Russia. It was only fifty-five miles at its closest point and there are two islands in between, to break up the journey if necessary.

He was a skilled artisan and engineer so when he needed something, he built it. When he left the snows he fashioned wheels to replace the skids on his sled. When he had to cross water he would build a boat. As his tools and clothes wore out he made new ones.

Without the consumption of mince pies and sherry, coupled with all the physical activity, Nick had become hard and lean. He would walk through the summers and when autumn came around he'd find a nice spot near a river, build himself a log cabin and hunker down for the winter. If he liked the location and there were plenty of fish in the river, then he might stay there for a few years.

Funny thing about the fish, they lived on in the rivers and the oceans. Maybe because it was an airborne disease that had killed everyone off and they lived underwater. Who knew? He just knew that they tasted fine after a diet of nuts and berries.

Millennia passed as he made his way across the continents. Nick didn't stray too much into the southern hemisphere, too hot for his liking. He was a temperate climate man. He liked pleasant summers and cold, snowy winters in the craggy mountains in places like Scandinavia, Canada and the American Rocky Mountains, as opposed to the Great Plains of America or the frozen tundra of Asia.

Over the centuries he noticed that the birds and some animals such as deer and bison were reappearing. Presumably the herds had been hidden away in some valley where the plague never reached. He checked those valleys for signs of humanity but there were none. Venison tasted nice again though.

***

One day in early spring, as Nick sat fishing in the rivers swollen by the melting snow, he felt an old, familiar tingle run down his spine. He hadn't felt that tingle for a couple of thousand years but he knew straight away what it was. Life! Not just the animals that were slowly re-populating the world, he could sense them but they were a kind of low-level background buzz that he could ignore. This was different, this was intelligent life!

He was currently in what had once been Greenland and the call came from the east, over the sea. He knew that east of him was Iceland and then continental Europe. At this distance he couldn't tell where the tingle was coming from but he would find out.

Nick spent the next few weeks making sure his boat was still sea-worthy and stocking it with supplies. Satisfied at last, he set sail. He reached Iceland and skirted the coastline, his senses telling him that the island wasn't his final destination. The call still came to him from the east. Landing only for fresh water and some more fishing, he set off for Europe.

He made landfall in one of the fjords of Norway. Packing everything into a rucksack he set off overland, "following his nose" as it were.

After he had crossed Norway and entered into Sweden, by his estimation, he arrived at his destination. It was a clearing in the forest, surrounded by rocks. He briefly scouted the area but saw no one or nothing unusual. He knew he was in the right area so he decided to make camp and wait to see what would happen. He didn't want to sit right on top of the site so he retreated a little further up the mountain to a spot where he could keep an eye on it. He found himself a cave, tracked down a water supply and blocked the front of the cave with logs, to keep out the elements.

Then he sat down to wait for whoever or whatever would show themselves. As he waited he took out his knife and whittled pieces of wood, to pass the time and contain his nervousness.

It took many days before he saw them but one night just as he was going to bed he looked down on the clearing and saw movement. A couple of beings, humanoid shaped, had entered the clearing. They cautiously made forays into the forest, returning with food, nuts and berries presumably, always returning to the clearing together, as if afraid to be parted.

Nick left his cave and crept down to get a clearer look at them. He had no fear that they would see him; he had been visiting people's houses all round the world for hundreds of years and had never once been spotted.

There were two, no wait, three of them, there was a young one clinging to the chest of one of the creatures. Nick assumed that it was a family unit, a father, a mother and their baby. Not very tall, they would have come up to Nick's waist if he stood next to them. And they were hairy, like chimpanzees, only they walked upright, not scoot around on all fours like monkeys tend to do. They had big, round eyes and, he realised, pointed ears! He wondered if they were an offshoot of the elves that had worked with him at the North Pole.

Once they had gathered enough food they went back to the biggest rock, which Nick realised wasn't just a rock but the entrance to a cave. They sat there eating their food while he studied them. Although he couldn't hear what they were saying, he saw that they talked to each other, so they obviously had some sort of rudimentary intelligence if they had a spoken language.

He'd seen no sign of them during the daytime so perhaps they only came out at night. If that cave was the entrance to an underground maze of caves and tunnels, maybe there was a whole tribe of them living underground. That might explain why they had such big eyes and only came out when it was dark. It might also account for how they survived the plague.

Why were there only the three of them outside the cave? Where were the others? They surely couldn't be the only ones; they wouldn't have survived this long if they were. Nick wondered if these three had decided to risk venturing out into the world, but their tribe dare not follow them. He had only sensed them recently, so maybe this couple were more adventurous than the others and he'd only registered them when they came above ground.

After a while they settled down to sleep, still in the safety of the cave mouth. The father figure cuddled up to the mother with the child secure between them.

Nick returned to his cave to pick up a few items and thought through his next move. As yet he hadn't seen any dangerous creatures in this new world but he knew it was only a matter of time. When there is plenty of prey this would eventually lead to the rise of predators.

Not if he had anything to do with it! He would look after this little family unit, protect them as he had always tried to protect mankind, and once they had shown the rest of the tribe that it was safe outside and they joined them, he would protect them too.

He crept into the mouth of the cave and placed a carving of a wooden deer into the child's hands. Then he covered the three of them with a blanket. Quietly he left the cave and made his way back up the mountain. As he did he smiled.

It was coming again. It may take centuries and it would surely be called something else but the season of goodwill and the giving of presents would be born again and he would be there to help it along.

'Christmas' would come again.

LAST REQUEST

Hazel McLoughlin

The coffin lay open on the table. The wake was drawing to a close. Men, awkward in Sunday suits, shook her hand and said, "Sorry-for-your-trouble," good-byes.

"Ye'll be paying heed to Joe's last request then, Mary?"

"Yes, Father, I will indeed."

She stood at the door of the stone farmhouse and watched them make their way down the rutted lane. From under the bed she took the butter-box and looked at the money. There'd be plenty of room for it alongside Joe's shrunken body. Everyone knew it was what he wanted.

She walked with Father Malone from the freshly filled grave.

"He'll be the happy man now that ye've buried him with his money."

The question was implicit.

"I did indeed, Father. Sure I wrote him a cheque."

ABOUT THE AUTHORS

Sue Tompkinson

The Ghost Walk, On Dementia, Rest Home Rhythm and Blues, The Family House

I'm a retired secretary who has traded business correspondence for stories, poems and various other creative scribblings. Great fun!

Tony Rattigan

Much Ado about Nothing, Eternal Night-Rising Dawn, No, That's Spelt G-U-I-D-O

Despite being retired and of pensionable age, Tony still hasn't decided what he's going to be when he grows up.

Mark Fletcher

The Grand National, The Commute

A late thirties, full-time grafter, and part-time daydreamer, who one day decided to put the latter to good use.

Catherine Wilson

Pie Dance

When I was at school my mum asked me what I'd like to be when I grew up.

I said, 'A famous writer, a singer or a long distance lorry driver.'

Dad scotched the LDLD idea – 'You can scribble any time, so get a job,' and my sisters and brother sang better than me.

I became a nurse, an artist and a mother and wrote in secret.

Still a mother and semi-retired art restorer, I've 'come out' with my 'scribbles' and have had a few things published.

Not famous, can't hold a tune, but I can write. BULKINGTON WRITERS have given me confidence, and I still have the LDLD idea at the back of my mind.

Hazel McLoughlin

Bookworm, Francophone, Last Request, Rogue Element

Hazel McLoughlin was born and educated in Ireland.

She has worked as a teacher in Africa, Ireland and England, latterly in a school for children with Special Educational Needs.

She has always enjoyed language in all its forms and has been fortunate, through travel, to encounter it in different cultures and countries and to find encouragement on a weekly basis to put pen to paper.

Mark Kockelbergh

McGonagall's Ghost, Orpheus in the Underground, Cold White Horse

Having wanted to write for more than forty years, I finally wrote my first short story ten years ago.

I don't limit myself to any particular genre but write about whatever interests me.

A (very) recently retired Chartered Accountant, I will be moving from Nuneaton soon to live with my wife next to the beach near Liverpool to spend more time with our three daughters.

Jean Busby

Autumn, Barney the Bassett Hound, Lovers Reunited, The House, The Theatre Visit

I have loved writing these stories. Enjoy readers.

Chris Allen

Rain, Encounters, Transgression

Chris, unfortunately, still has to work but manages, in his spare time, to annoy the neighbours playing guitar badly and finds time to write the occasional short story. He is the author of a wildly unsuccessful short work, Threads (available on Kindle) but, despite this, still harbours grand literary ambitions!

June Bradley

A Tranquil Sea, A Path through the Wood, A Ptolemaic Tale

Writing was an itch I had never got around to scratching. So when the big 'five 0' slithered over the horizon my husband casually lobbed a North Warwickshire College evening class prospectus at me and said, "There you go – if you don't try it now you'll never know."

So in 2004 I joined Diane Lindsay's Creative Writing class and with the help of a speech recognition package I'm still scribbling.

Ian Collier

One Night in Bangor, In a Wide Open Space

Ian writes some stuff including Nuneaton Noir.

BULKINGTON WRITERS

Bulkington Writers is partway between a class and a writer's circle and meets on Wednesdays at 7-9 in Bulkington Village Centre's Garden Room. All levels of expertise are welcome and the first taster session is free. There is an email group and lots of support and encouragement for newcomers, plus positive and helpful criticism for more experienced writers

Printed in Great Britain
by Amazon

11505721R00108